SUMMER AWAKENING

by

Eric Malpass

Dales Large Print Books
Long Preston, North Yorkshire,
BD23 4ND, England.

British Library Cataloguing in Publication Data.

Malpass, Eric
    Summer awakening.

    A catalogue record of this book is
    available from the British Library

    ISBN   1-84262-328-1 pbk

Dales Large Print is an imprint of Library Magna Books Ltd.

Printed and bound in Great Britain by
T.J. (International) Ltd., Cornwall, PL28 8RW

SUMMER AWAKENING

Tales from the Pentecost Family.

A long hot summer in the Pentecost house promises the usual mayhem. Gaylord manages to persuade his mother to allow Christine, a German au pair, to stay. With the help of the pretty fräulein he discovers his awakening interest in the fairer sex. Momma notices that other people seem to appreciate Christine's teutonic charms too, while ten-year-old Amanda falls hopelessly in love with Gaylord's friend Roger. Before long, Gaylord is wishing the heady days of summer would never end, while for Momma the first hint of autumn cannot come soon enough.

To our beloved Ruth Liepman

CHAPTER 1

Gaylord Pentecost came back from his summer holidays in Germany. He said, 'Mother, you know you said you wanted an au pair girl?'

'Did I, darling?'

'Yes. You remember?'

'I do now. It was about ten years ago. You were a little boy and Amanda was a babe in arms.'

Gaylord did wish that Mother, whenever he had a Dramatic Announcement to make, wouldn't somehow edge him off centre stage. He said, slightly deflated, 'Well, I've got you one.' He gave her his charming, boyish smile.

May said, 'But darling, I don't want one. In those days, yes. Now, no.' And she thought: what mother with an adolescent son *would* introduce an au pair girl into her home? As soon lower a match into a petrol can to find out if it was empty.

Gaylord felt discouraged. And he did wish people would make up their minds. He said, 'But I've *asked* her.'

'Then you'll just have to *un*ask her, Gaylord.' May's voice had taken on an edge.

She was an amiable woman, but she knew her own mind. And she wasn't filling the house with nubile Fräuleins. Like most educated but untravelled English, she imagined that the female population of Germany consisted largely of Rhine Maidens, Loreleis, Brunhildes and Daughters of the Erl King. 'You'll have to unask her,' she said again.

Gaylord said, 'I *can't*. It wouldn't be – honourable.'

Oh Lord, thought May. Her son had always clung like a leech to a principle. And how much she admired him for it! But it did make life difficult. She sighed, switched off her electric iron, sat down. This was going to take time, as well as tact. 'Tell me about her,' she said.

'Her name's Christine. She plays the piano and tennis, and she's a *superb* horsewoman. She's not bad looking, either, for a girl.'

'Really? If she can also manage a bit of cooking and cleaning, she sounds an ideal au pair. But–' May's glance hardened. 'She's not coming, Gaylord.'

The pleasant young face was pink under its sunburn. 'But I said she could, Mother.'

'Then you had no business to say she could. How dare you commit me in that way? You'll write and stop her.'

'I can't.'

'Why not?'

'I don't know her address.'

8

She looked at him furiously. 'Gaylord, you fool! You invite some girl whose address you don't even know to come and live in my house–?'

'Oh, I know *where* she lives. I've been there. It's some Schloss in Bavaria. But – there are no end of Schlosses in Bavaria.'

She stared at him in exasperation. 'You actually said she could come?'

'Yes.' He was looking as near sulky as Gaylord could look. 'You did say you wanted one.'

'Ten years ago, for heaven's sake.'

'Well, I didn't know you'd changed your mind.' *La donna e mobile* was clearly the thought uppermost in his brain.

She said, clutching at straws, 'Anyway, her parents would never let her come without writing to me first. Why, I might be anybody.'

'I think they will, Mother. Christine says her mother is very strict and particular. But she told her you were a cousin of the Queen's.'

May wasn't often lost for words. But she was now. She just stared.

Gaylord explained. 'She read in a book that everyone in England is at least a fourteenth cousin of the Queen. It – it sounds feasible,' he finished lamely.

'I believe it's quite true. But did she point out to her parents that it's an honour I share

9

with the other twenty million English women?'

'I think perhaps she didn't.'

May was silent. Then she said quietly, 'And you talk to me of honour.'

Gaylord said quickly, 'But she *is* honourable, Mother. If you met her you'd see that.' Almost to himself, he said, 'She – sort of – radiates honour.'

May, curiously, believed him. But then, she always believed Gaylord.

Grandpa barged in, saw their glum faces. 'Hello. What's up with you two?' If there was an argument going, Grandpa liked to be there, demanding explanations, adding to the confusion, confounding the issues, exacerbating the opponents. He firmly believed that, when he was gone, people would remember him fondly as 'old John Pentecost the Peacemaker.'

May said, 'Gaylord's arranged to have an au pair girl shipped out from Germany.'

Grandpa's trim white moustache bristled. 'Then you can damn well ship her back. Not having any au pair girls in this house. Sit around all day playing records and pushing their hair out of their eyes.'

'Christine doesn't,' Gaylord said hotly.

The old man stabbed a finger at his daughter-in-law. 'Stop her coming, May. Jack Walters had one. He found her smoking pot in his favourite Dunhill.' He blanched at the thought.

In a flat voice May said, 'We can't stop her coming. Gaylord doesn't know her address.' She rose, and went up to her husband's study. Jocelyn Pentecost's lean and anxious features brightened at her entrance. 'Hello, old girl. Could you type this letter for me?'

'Yes.' Then she told him about the au pair. He sat playing with his pen. She said, 'What worries me is that he'll probably go and fall in love with her. An unknown girl, from Central Europe. And coming here, to be under the same roof. And – I'd always rather hoped – he and little Liz Bunting might–'

Amanda was working on the window ledge. (Daddy thought she was helping him by punching binding holes in the typescript of his new novel, but what she was also doing was making confetti for the wedding of her doll Cleo to her Teddy Bear; Teddy having decided, as she told her astonished grand-father, to make an honest woman of Cleo.)

Now she looked at her mother with sudden interest and even alarm. Amanda didn't want any competition from teenage female foreigners, thank you very much. It wasn't only that she might lose her dear companion Gaylord. She loved, with all the single-minded devotion of a ten-year-old, Gaylord's splendid friend Roger Miles. And the fewer teenage girls therc were around Roger, the better Amanda would be pleased. She had noticed that young men of seventeen unaccountably lost interest in ten-year-olds when girls of their own age were around. Besides, she too had quite decided that Gaylord must marry Liz. She gave the punch a sharp bang with her little fist; and took a dreadful oath that, if Gaylord *did* get his girl over here she, Amanda, would get her back again in two shakes of a nanny goat's tail.

Jocelyn didn't often see his serene wife so upset. He gave her his slow, friendly smile. 'She may never arrive,' he said. 'I believe German parents are much stricter–'

The front door bell rang. May went down, opened the door. A girl stood on the step. Her features were largely hidden by enormous sunglasses, and by a cascade of hair as sleek and warmly coloured as a chestnut newly prised from its shell. Nevertheless, May had an impression there was beauty here – but not the blonde, statuesque beauty of the German. Clearly, she thought with relief, this was not Gaylord's Nordic Goddess.

The girl said, 'Mrs Pentecost? How do you do? I am Christine Haldt, and I have come to be your au pair girl. I cook French and Italian dishes, but not yet English. I hope you have a piano and a tennis court and that there are riding stables nearby. I know many amusing and interesting stories of my Onkel Willi.' She shook hands warmly...

CHAPTER 2

It could all be said to have begun on a summer's evening in the orchard of the Pentecost farmhouse, at the beginning of the summer holidays.

Charles Bunting had driven over to paint a picture of the river valley from the orchard. The fact that his daughter Liz decided to accompany him had, of course, nothing to do with the fact that Gaylord Pentecost was due home for the school holidays that evening. Or so Liz hoped that everyone would believe.

Charles Bunting had a tremendous reputation as an artist, a 1935 open Rolls Royce, and an artistic temperament.

Jocelyn Pentecost did not envy Charles his reputation or his vintage Rolls, because he was always sensibly content with what he himself could achieve. But he did envy him his artistic temperament. He felt that he himself, as an author, was *entitled* to an artistic temperament. But it was a luxury he wasn't allowed. You couldn't be married to May, *and* throw tantrums. You'd just be laughed out of court. You couldn't live in the same house as his sturdy old father, and give way to emotional outbursts. You couldn't, he thought miserably, get away with *anything* when your ten-year-old daughter beheld you with the fearful clarity of innocence, eager to announce to the world your slightest deviation from the psychological norm.

The sun was westering; a golden orange caught in the apple-tree boughs. Amanda was on an old swing. She moved gently. She was, for once, as restful as the pendulum of a grandfather clock. Charles Bunting jabbed his brush at his painting, as irritably as a farmyard hen pecking scraps. The rest sprawled in their garden chairs in the long grass of the orchard. Grandpa watched his cigar smoke wreath up among the leaves; twist, curl away to mingle with the unlit stars. May leafed through a magazine, a serene smile about her lips. Charles' daughter Liz gazed anxiously at the river road – the *empty* river road. Jocelyn watched them all, lazily, thinking: what Turgenev, Chekhov would have made of this placid, sunset scene! What turmoil would they have uncovered in those gently beating hearts! And what can *I* see? Nothing. Only hearts at peace, under an English heaven.

May said, 'I thought Gaylord would have been here by now.'

Grandpa, who was enjoying his cigar, said, 'Time enough, May.'

She turned on him in mock surprise,

14

'What do you mean, old man. Don't you want to see your grandson?'

'Not particularly. The moment that lad arrives you women'll be dashing about like slaves in a bally harem. I shan't be able to finish my cigar. Even the sun won't be able to go down in peace.'

Liz Bunting looked even more anxiously at the river road. Still empty! Suppose something *dreadful* had happened to him! She would die! Yet she knew she would not die. Life was more cruel than that. She would live on, leave school, take a job, become an ageing spinster in a world and a life empty of sunlight and colour, empty of everything.

'Damn the sun. It won't keep still,' snarled Bunting.

'Your name's not Joshua,' said May.

He turned, and looked at her thoughtfully. She grinned at him. He did not smile back, but went on with his painting. She wondered whether she had annoyed him. She wasn't worried about it. She liked old Charles. But if you never said anything he might take amiss, you'd never speak.

Amanda's swing slowed, stopped. She said, 'If I were Mr Bunting I should want to paint Mummy. Very much.'

Charles stood back from his painting, looked at her with irritation and surprise. 'I *do* want to paint her very much.'

'Good Lord,' said Jocelyn. Old May was

jolly good looking, he knew. But he hadn't thought of her as being in the Mona Lisa class. He pondered. May, in evening dress, with a special hair-do by Madame Teresa of Shepherd's Warning, hanging over the fireplace in a gilt frame? It really was an attractive idea. 'You – wouldn't really have a go, would you, old chap?'

Charles Bunting had impatient and hungry features, accentuated by a black, down-curling moustache. And smouldering grey eyes. Now the eyes flickered into life like blown embers. 'Of course I will. If May's agreeable.'

'Once had a fellow in to do your mother,' Grandpa warned. 'Made a dreadful hash of it.'

But to everyone's surprise, May said, 'I don't think so, Charles. Thank you all the same.' She was smiling. But there was a stubborn set to her chin.

'Oh, come on, old girl,' said Jocelyn. 'I'd love to have you hanging over the mantel-piece.' He was quite carried away with the idea.

Grandpa said: 'She looked like Dan Leno in pantomime by the time he'd finished with her.'

'I just thought Mr Bunting would like to, that's all,' said Amanda. She watched them all through her wide-set, narrow eyes. Her eyes were hidden by their long lashes. But

16

the area around them would suddenly suffuse with amusement or compassion, or love – or with a devastating understanding of human frailty.

'I *would* like to, dammit. Oh come on, May. Stop playing hard to get. I'll do you sewing, by the fire.'

Jocelyn said, 'I'd rather thought – that blue evening dress, with one of Mabel Higgins' – Madame Teresa's – hairdos.'

'And the Garter ribbon across her bosom, I suppose,' Charles said witheringly.

Liz Bunting said, '*Do* let Daddy paint you, Mrs Pentecost.' It was a wonderful idea. Liz thought Mrs Pentecost was the most beautiful woman, as well as the nicest person, she had ever met. Ever since she had lost her own mother May Pentecost had been friend, elder sister, mother, according to the girl's particular need.

May only said, 'If Gaylord doesn't come soon, I–' But at that moment Amanda cried, 'It's him. Look.' And she leapt from the swing and did three cartwheels in rapid succession.

'He,' corrected Jocelyn. He was ignored. Everyone was watching the road, which was no longer empty, but now contained a schoolboy riding a bicycle.

Grandpa had been right. Gaylord wasn't even here yet, but the peace was shattered. May and Jocelyn were gathering up their magazines, Charles Bunting was putting away his paints, even the sun was dipping to the horizon; Amanda was still cartwheeling, and uttering shrill, bird-like cries of delight. And Liz Bunting sat, bunched tight in her chair, looking as though breathing was very difficult, as indeed it was.

She wanted, she longed to run to the gate, to see whether he really *could* be as handsome, and as nice, as she remembered him. To see how the thirteen-week school term had changed him – for her, thirteen weeks of long, empty days, days of smouldering heat and high-climbing thunderheads, of the swift hiss of rain on summer grass. The summer days, lost, grey as winter since Gaylord was not here. And now – he was back. And she must not run to greet him. She must wait, in the background, until *he* sought *her* out. She must sit here, quiet as the summer evening, absorbed in *Woman's Own*, until, at last, a shadow from the dying sun fell across her magazine, and she looked up and said, in casual surprise, 'Why, young Gaylord. You startled me.'

It was hard. But it was the way of women. Yet at the same time her heart cried out: 'He's back. For six joyful weeks. And Mrs Pentecost has asked me to go to Wales with them again. So we shall be together. As it was in the days when I was young Liz and he was young Gaylord, building a barrage of sand to keep out Cardigan Bay; before, unaccountably, and in the twinkling of an eye, he became my sun, my moon and my stars, my summer days. And yet for him I stayed young Liz.'

But Amanda had no such inhibitions. She tore across the paddock, into the house, out into the drive, hurled herself at a sunburnt schoolboy. 'Gaylord! We're in the orchard, and Mr Bunting wants to paint Mummy and she won't let him, isn't it strange, I think it's some sort of psychological block, don't you? Did you get into the Eleven?'

Gaylord Pentecost was wearing a school blazer and flannels, and a school cap tilted forward over his gravely smiling face. Far more important, he wore the casual majesty of a member of the Upper Fifth. But even members of the Upper Fifth have been known, when no one was looking, to unbend for kid sisters. And Gaylord unbent now. He hoisted the crowing Amanda on to his back and galloped into the orchard.

'Gaylord!' cried May, holding out her hands. 'How lovely!'

He took her hands, swinging them to and fro. 'Hello Mum.' He stopped and kissed the top of her head. 'I say, you're not half going grey.'

'I know.'

'Henry Bartlett says *his* mother's hair's still as black as the day she was seventeen.

It's something she gets from Boots. I'll ask the name of it if you like.' He perched on the edge of a chair, throwing a delighted Amanda off on to the grass.

'Hello, Dad, Grandfather. Hello, Mr Bunting. If you paint my mother will she have two eyes in one side of her head, and a large hole through her middle?'

Charles Bunting looked put out. May said quietly, 'Darling, that was a bit rude.'

'Sorry, Mother. Sorry, Mr Bunting.'

'I dare say he's a bit over-excited,' said Amanda with great understanding. 'Adrenalin or something.'

Charles Bunting said, stiffly, 'It will be a study in serenity and repose, young Gaylord.'

'Like Whistler's Mother,' said May with a sudden giggle. She was cross with herself, but she couldn't help it. Charles was so *prickly*.

Charles slapped a brush angrily against his palette. On that still evening, it made a crack like an air gun being fired. May said, 'Sorry, Charles. That was unpardonable.'

He grunted. Then, surprisingly, gave her a sudden wolfish grin.

Gaylord sat slapping his school cap against his knee. Liz, while concentrating on *Women's Own*, managed to watch him out of the corner of an eye. She was the only one he hadn't noticed yet. She wanted to die. She wanted to run and fling herself into the river.

He'd *have* to notice her then. But would he? She wanted to go and stamp angrily on his foot and say, 'Remember me – young Liz?' But she wasn't the type for dramatics and she knew he'd just grin and stamp back.

But if she thought her cup was already full, she soon found the teapot of misery wasn't empty yet. For Gaylord said, 'Oh, Mum, you know Roger Miles? Actually, he's leaving. But he *was* School Captain, *and* Captain of Cricket and Captain of Rugger.'

'What about him?' Amanda asked eagerly. Her ten-year-old heart almost burst at this mention of her beloved.

But May knew that when Gaylord spoke in this throwaway manner she was supposed to be impressed. 'Goodness!' she said, 'Does he feed on ambrosia?'

Mother and son grinned at each other. 'No. He has the ordinary school meals. But – well, his Uncle Frank's taking some Venture Scouts to Germany for August, and he's asked Miles to go with them and take a friend, and – and Miles has asked me.' He paused, drinking in the wonder of it. 'It's a bit super, actually.'

May knew her son. She knew that for him it was a shade better than being asked to a week's shooting at Sandringham by Prince Philip. Nevertheless, there was the family to consider – that loose-knit, tight-knit group of individuals known as the Pentecosts. So she said, 'Darling, we're going to Wales. Besides–'

'Oh, Mummy, can *I* go?' cried Amanda. Germany with her two favourite men!

'No, dear,' said May.

''Course not,' said Gaylord. 'It isn't the Brownies.'

'Germany?' said Grandpa. 'What the devil do you want to go to Germany for?' He could never understand the family traipsing off to Wales, even. But Germany? What was wrong with England, for heaven's sake?

Gaylord said, with just a suggestion of wistfulness, 'It does sound rather super, Mum. And it's only five quid. Or is it fifty?'

Oh God, make them say no, Liz was praying. *Let them say he's got to come to Wales.*

'You'd better ask your father,' said May.

Gaylord thought this was potty. *He* knew who made the decisions. His father always said, quite frankly, the hell with family problems, he'd got quite enough fictional ones, thank you very much. Still, protocol. 'Can I, Dad?' he asked.

'Can you what?' asked Jocelyn, looking at his son as though seeing him for the first time. He was far away. The sun was a golden orange, and little orangey-pink clouds floated about the sky, lovely and innocent as the cherubim; all about them the soft air was suffused with colour – blue and pink and orange. And someone had mentioned

22

Germany, bringing a line of poetry, half forgotten – "'*Kennst du das Land, wo die Zitronen blühn–?*'" How did it go on? 'Can you what?' he asked again.

'Go to Germany, Dad. For August.'

'Don't see why not. You'll need a passport.'

'I got one at school.'

'I think you're absolutely foul, Gaylord,' said Amanda.

May thought: holidays in Wales, with the children young; bare, sturdy limbs, salt-caked, the harsh cuff of brine, laughter, the bright mornings, running barefoot where sand met sea, the lamplit evenings with the kids in bed and the Welsh rain pounding on the Welsh roof, and dear Jocelyn sprawled with his pipe and his book, content. Holidays in Wales! And now, can I go to Germany? Five pounds or fifty, can't remember. There'd been a time, she thought, when fifty pounds would have rented the cottage for a year. But that was foolishness. Her world was changing. Her old, loved world was disintegrating like a sand castle before the approaching tide. And her family, the strong, united family she had moulded and protected, was changing with it. Her young man of a son was no longer content to splash in an icy British sea, nor must she expect him to be. Her world had grown up, was growing old, even. Her son thought she needed something from

Boots for her hair. And Charles wanted to paint her as a homely wife, and she didn't want him to. And she, who usually saw her own motives with frankness and clarity, could not say why she did not want him to. She looked at the dying sun, at a cloud of gnats, dancing away the last hours of their little day. She, who told herself proudly that she was never depressed unless there was reason to be depressed, felt a vague and unaccountable weight about her shoulders. Could it be her forty years, Jocelyn's forty years? The fact that the child to whom her body had once been everything – food, warmth, comfort, love – was now a sturdy, young Englishman for whom even her tight little island was not enough? She said, 'Amanda and Liz will miss you, Gaylord.'

Amanda nodded vigorously. Liz called out, bravely, 'That's all right, Mrs Pentecost. *We* shall be all right, shan't we, Mandy?'

Gaylord looked up at her voice. 'Hi, young Liz,' he called cheerfully. He strolled across, and tipped her straw hat over her eyes.

At the warmth and friendliness of his greeting, Liz almost swooned with pleasure. 'Hello, Gaylord,' she breathed reverently. She put her hat straight, so that she could give him an adoring smile.

To her delight he threw himself down on the grass beside her chair, began chewing a grass blade, grinning up at her. But before either of them could say anything Jocelyn called, 'Gaylord, do you know that thing of Goethe's about lemons? "Kennst du das Land–?" I'm stuck for the second line.'

'"Im dunkeln Laub die Gold – Orangen glühn",' called Gaylord. He scrambled to his feet, went back to his father. 'It's jolly good, isn't it?'

'Yes. Thanks. I'd have been awake half the night trying to remember that second line.'

A breeze of evening came and ruffled the surface of the river, threw the gnats into disarray with its murmur of *memento mori*, lifted the page of Liz's *Women's Own*. May said, 'I think we should go in.' Charles Bunting said, 'Come on, Liz. Time to be getting back.' John Pentecost ground his cigar into the grass. Half an inch of it, wasted. And how many more cigars would he smoke, in his orchard, before cigars and orchards and earth and sun, and all comfort, were extinguished? Not so many, now. *Lord Rameses of Egypt sighed Because a summer evening passed–* Jocelyn strolled across. 'Want a hand, Father?' The old man glared up at him from his deck chair. 'Of course I don't want a hand, dammit. I'm not decrepit.' He struggled to his feet. And it *was* a struggle. But that was nothing to do with age. It was just that they made deck chairs so low nowadays.

May slipped her arms into Gaylord's. 'Nice to have you back, darling.'

'Nice to be back, Mum.'

A desperately cheerful cry came across the grass. 'Goodbye, Gaylord.'

Mother and son turned. Liz stood by the open Rolls. She waved, smiled wanly. She looked like a girl who would find all heaven in a kiss. But there were no kisses this summer eve. 'So long, Liz,' called Gaylord, and went his happy way. The engine of the Rolls purred into life. The car overtook them, as they trekked back to the house: the sturdy old man, stamping along at the close of one more day from his little store; Jocelyn, slightly drunk with the beauty of sunset and countryside and poetry; May and her son, happy to be together; Amanda, still cartwheeling joyously because her brother had come. Charles Bunting touched the horn, and gathered speed. The car swept down the river road away from them. It cast a long shadow.

May squeezed Gaylord's arm. 'You'll be careful in Germany?'

'I will, Mother.' He grinned. 'I'll tell Miles' uncle not to do more than thirty on the Autobahn.'

'I didn't mean the Autobahn. I was thinking of the women. They're very beautiful, I hear.'

'Girls!' He laughed scornfully. 'Oh, they're all right when you're kids. But a chap's got more important things – cricket, rugger–'

She smiled. 'Of course, dear.' But she thought: don't leave it too long, my son. Kisses can lose their sweetness with the years. And Liz would give her right hand for a kiss.

But she knew, in her heart, poor Liz was unlikely to get one.

She was still vaguely depressed when, later that evening, she tucked Amanda into bed. 'Night-night, my darling.' She turned away, began tidying the dressing table. 'By the way, how did you know Mr Bunting would like to paint my portrait?'

Her head was turned away from her child. But she knew those candid eyes were watching her every movement. Amanda said thoughtfully, 'I don't know, Mummy. I thought he might be in love with you. But he *couldn't* be, could he? 'Cos you're married.'

'No dear, of course he couldn't,' said May, looking and sounding quite calm. But as soon as she was away from that frank stare she recognized, immediately, that what her child said was true. And she laughed: a dry, angry little laugh. She, who was Jocelyn's, who was Jocelyn's till all the seas ran dry, being loved by another man! It was ridiculous! And she should put a stop to it at once. But how could she, when it was all surmise, perhaps even conceit on her part?

But she thought: Amanda spotted it. Amanda knew, the little devil. How blind

I've been! And how long has it been going on? Since Rachel died? That's it. He formed a sentimental feeling for me, to compensate for the loss of his wife. And of course he's a man of honour. He'd die rather than let either Jocelyn or me have an inkling of his feelings. Poor Charles! She tried to feel sympathy. Yet, to her surprise, could feel only a sense of affront; and, at the same time, an almost arrogant satisfaction that she deplored but that nevertheless lifted her depression. Perhaps she wasn't doing so badly without that stuff from Boots, after all.

But then the thought struck her like a blow: why do I assume he'll go on being a man of honour? The fact that I take honour for granted among *my* menfolk has nothing to do with Charles. She was suddenly uneasy.

When at last she climbed into bed, she said gravely: 'I had a strange thought today, Jocelyn.'

'Did you, old girl? Look, can you wait a moment? Just got to clean my teeth.' He went into the bathroom. He came back. 'That toothpaste. The one with the new wonder additive. It tastes like saddle soap.'

'I've never tasted saddle soap.'

Did he detect a drop in temperature? He thought hard. He remembered. A strange thought! He said, with exaggerated eagerness, 'Now then. What's this strange thought of yours?'

'Well, it sounds terribly conceited. But – I suddenly wondered whether Charles Bunting was in love with me.'

'Old Charles? 'Course he is. Been in love with you for years.'

She jerked up in bed. 'You mean – you *knew*?'

He was beginning to look smug. 'I suppose we writers have an instinct for that sort of thing.'

She sat, hugging her knees. At last she said. 'I began to think he'd told you. I thought perhaps you two had had a good old heart-to-heart about it.'

'No, no.' He sounded rather shocked. 'Wouldn't be quite the thing, would it, May?'

'I don't know. I wouldn't have thought falling in love with another man's wife was quite the thing, personally.'

'No. But of course chaps do. And you *can* be quite attractive, old girl.'

'Thanks.'

She sat silent, rubbing her chin across her knees. 'But I'm forty, Jocelyn.' It was almost a wail. 'Gaylord thinks I ought to dye my hair.'

He looked at her thoughtfully, and shook his head. 'No. Wouldn't suit you. Growing old gracefully's more your style, May.'

Again she was silent. Then: 'I suppose so,' she said. She lay down, sighed. 'Jocelyn?'

'Yes?'

'You don't mind? About old Charles?'

He laughed heartily. 'My dear May! I hope I'm sufficiently civilized–' He slid into bed, yawned.

'Yes,' she said. 'I hadn't looked at it that way. Good night.'

'Good night,' he said.

But she lay awake, thinking: Is *he* growing middle-aged, too? Middle-aged, and solemn, and – pompous? Her Jocelyn, who had always so delighted her with his wry, amused, self-deprecating humour? *I hope I'm sufficiently civilized–?*

Middle age, here we come! she thought glumly, wide-awake. She said, 'We'll have to give Liz the chance of withdrawing from the Welsh holiday. It'll be quiet for her without Gaylord.'

'Oh, she'll be all right. She'll take Amanda off our hands. And she's a great help about the cottage.'

She turned to face him. And said, slowly, 'You know, Jocelyn, if you don't watch it you'll soon be as selfish as your father.'

He lifted his head from the pillow, gave her a startled look. '*Is* Father selfish?' He pondered. 'Yes. Do you know, old girl, I do believe he can be. Clever of you to spot it.'

'Thanks,' she said. He lay silent, absolutely still. He had a feeling May was in a rather tetchy mood tonight. He'd be very relieved when she dropped off.

Charles and Liz Bunting came home. They put the car in the garage, walked back to their cottage. Liz found she was trembling. She always was, when she had been driven by Daddy.

But it wasn't only Daddy's appalling driving. It was seeing Gaylord again – for a few bittersweet minutes. It was learning that Gaylord was going to be away in Germany for most of the holidays. It was learning that Gaylord wasn't coming to Wales. It was grey disappointment, at an age when a month ahead seems a lifetime ahead.

Charles slipped an arm about his daughter's shoulders. He and she had been very close since his wife died. 'What about a frizzle?' he said. 'Ham and eggs.'

'And sausages,' she said.

'And tomatoes.'

'And fried bread.'

'You put the things on the table,' he said, 'I'll toil over the hot stove.'

In the kitchen, breaking eggs, he said, 'I'm sorry young Gaylord's not going to Wales with you, Liz.' His voice was, for him, gentle.

She felt the colour rush to her cheeks. How fortunate his back was towards her! 'Thanks, Daddy. But – it really doesn't matter.'

'Come off it. You love him dearly.'

She was overcome with embarrassment,

31

shame and amazement. After all her efforts to hide her feelings! 'How on earth did you know, Daddy?'

'My dear Liz, you can't hide young love. You might as well try to hide the Albert Hall with a dustsheet. I'll have English mustard.'

'Shall I open you some beer? I didn't know it was as obvious as all that.'

'Please. Pale Ale.' He scooped the contents of the frying pan on to two plates, carried them over to the kitchen table. They sat down. Outside the open cottage window, a calm afterglow lingered. But any scent of roses and lavender drifting in through the lattice was taken care of by the smell of ham and eggs and sausage rising up from their plates. Liz, who knew that anyone in her state of love should be revolted by the very thought of food, was bitterly disappointed in herself .Her mouth was watering, she just couldn't wait to begin. When she thought of the contempt with which Juliet would have regarded this meal, she hated and despised herself. And picked up her fork.

Charles ate in silence. He was a lonely, self-contained man. But not from choice. He would like a wife – but she would have to be like his own dear Rachel, a pearl of great price. And there were not many such. May Pentecost was one – but May Pentecost was not in the market. And he, who painted some of the loveliest women in England, knew that few of them had May's quality. And anyway, the few who had, had all been snapped up. He took a long drink of beer, put down his glass. He thrust aside his own loneliness and heartache, and gave his daughter his sudden, wolfish grin. And took up the conversation where they had left off. 'I hope it's not as obvious that I'm in love with his mother.'

She stared. She put down her fork. She went on staring.

He leaned across the table, squeezed her hand. 'Don't worry, my dear. It's something I can live with.'

She went on staring. Then she shivered violently.

'That kid knows,' he said. 'Young Amanda. So I thought you'd probably realized ages ago.'

She spoke at last. 'With – Mrs Pentecost? But – Mr Pentecost.'

'Oh, Lord,' he said. 'I'm a clumsy fool. It's – only a sentimental feeling, Liz. It'll never be anything more.'

She looked at him, long and hard. With love. But with a desperate effort at understanding. At last she said, as though seeking assurance, 'Of course. It – *couldn't* be anything more, could it, Father. Not with people like you and Mr and Mrs Pentecost.'

'Of course not,' he said.

Father and daughter looked at each other. Then, slowly, she began to eat her frizzle.

CHAPTER 3

A scholarly-looking man stood at the checkout barrier of the supermarket, rather desperately shoving groceries into a wire pram. On the other side of the barrier an elegant, serene-looking woman was paying the girl. Why, it's Gaylord's parents, thought Liz Bunting, blushing absurdly. Was Gaylord with them? She looked hurriedly round the shop. No Gaylord. But Mrs Pentecost looked up, saw her, and waved. So Liz went bravely up to the barrier and said, 'Hello, Mr Pentecost. Hello, Mrs Pentecost.'

Jocelyn looked at her rather wildly. This business of checking out groceries was something that always called for his most intense concentration. He was terrified that he would, by some maladroitness, hold up this queue of busy mums and dads, all grimly eager to get home and feed the kids and bath the baby and retile the kitchen and read the sports page and watch telly.

'Hello, Liz,' he said manhandling a frozen turkey into the wire pram. Much as he liked young Liz, he'd got to sort himself out before he could indulge in conversation.

But now Mrs Pentecost was coming up,

with her unruffled smile. 'Hello, dear,' she said, giving Liz's arm a squeeze. 'We were wanting to see you. Weren't we, Jocelyn?'

'Oh. Ah. Yes,' said Jocelyn, whose pram was intent on going southeast while Jocelyn wanted it to go southwest.

'We wondered whether you still felt like coming to Wales with us this year. Gaylord won't be with us, you know. So – we should quite understand.'

'I know, Mrs Pentecost. But – I'd love to come. Please.'

May heard the strain in the girl's voice, felt the emptiness of her response. And thought, as she had thought before: she's in love with my son. And she's going to get hurt. Because Gaylord will show her just about the same understanding he shows a Rugby football – and rather less affection. She said, gently, 'We'll try to give you a good time, my dear. But it may be rather dull for you.'

'It *won't* be dull, Mrs Pentecost.' Liz tried to give the impression that the presence or absence of Gaylord made no difference whatever to her. Jocelyn, whose wire basket had now come to terms, and who was proceeding towards the car park with all the aplomb of a Victorian nursemaid in Kensington Gardens, was quite taken in. Young Liz, he thought, enjoyed, and was flattered by, his company. She made him feel wise, fatherly and attractive in a mature sort of way. *She* wouldn't miss young Gaylord. But May knew better. 'I'm sorry Gaylord's off to Germany, Liz.'

'That's all right, Mrs Pentecost.' The smile was bright, too bright. Oh, the agony and the bravery of first love, thought May. *Patience on a monument, smiling at grief.* As usual, old William had hit the nail right on the head.

So Grandpa, as always when the family were away, went and stayed at his London Club, and felt his annual surprise at the way his fellow members had let themselves age during the year. He just didn't understand it. Must be his splendid constitution, his sensible way of life, that saved him from going the same sad way, he decided.

And the family went to Wales. And there was the cottage where not a plate, not a picture, not a rug, not a smell had changed in a twelvemonth. And there were lanes where nothing had changed in the slow centuries. And there were the empty shores where nothing had changed in a million years. And Liz walked lonely, her young mind awed and wrestling with the wonders of sunset, and solitude, and ocean; and of young love, deep and mysterious as the moaning sea itself and returned to the almost equal wonder of lamp lit kindliness, and the ability of love-torn youth to tuck in to hot pot and apple pie.

And Gaylord went off, calm on the surface but sizzling with excitement inside, to a land mass that stretched from Calais to Vladivostok, a land mass inhabited by people most of whom had never *been* to England, who didn't know cricket from rugger, Gilbert from Sullivan, Morecambe from Wise. He would never for one moment have admitted it, even to himself: but he really did rather wish his parents had been coming.

They ran the minibus down into the belly of the ship, and came on deck. And there were the decidedly off-white cliffs of Dover; and behind *them*, he knew – the little lanes, the rivers, the green fields of England. His mother, father, young Amanda would just be sitting down to lunch. The sunlight would be streaming through the windows. There would be an empty chair.

Hawsers were being cast off. England – docks, customs sheds, white cliffs and all – began imperceptibly but surely to drift away. Gaylord had a heavy, compressed feeling in his chest and stomach. He thought what a wonderful place England was. He even thought of his happy childhood in that noble land. He glanced quickly at his friend Henry Bartlett. Henry's eyes, behind their round spectacles, were also fixed rather desperately on those not-so-white cliffs. And, even as Gaylord looked, a tear ran down his friend's round, pink cheeks. It seemed that even

Venture Scouts were capable of that most harrowing malady – homesickness.

But, not apparently, ex School Captains. For Roger Miles slapped Gaylord cheerfully on the back and said. 'Thank the Lord. I couldn't wait to get away, could you, Pentecost?'

Gaylord gave him a wan smile, and said nothing. As a guest, he couldn't say he was wishing he hadn't come. And being slapped on the back by Miles was an honour he greatly appreciated. But he wasn't going to be disloyal to England. So he was silent, and Roger gave him a thoughtful look. There were times when he suspected young Pentecost of taking life a bit seriously.

But there was no homesickness left when they reached the Bavarian forests.

They had run across Europe. Names from dull geography books, from old history, had sprung into life on the signposts: Rheims, Verdun, Metz, the noble Rhine, Munich. They had heard men speaking French, German, not as in an exercise but as though they actually *thought* in these tiresome languages. They had run south from Munich, the road gleaming red and clean before them in the southern sun. And then, at last, they had seen them: dark, jagged, mysterious shapes floating in the sky, like sinister clouds; streaked with glinting ice and barred with snow, they saw as they came nearer. They ran on, awestruck, until the white majesties were all about them, and their valley was carpeted with firs.

They plunged into the forest, along a track that seemed to go on forever. They came to a clearing. It had a stream, an expanse of turf, a lofty wall of trees and, above that, watchful, unsleeping, a white fang of mountain. And here they camped.

On the first afternoon Roger Miles said to Gaylord, 'I don't know about you, Pentecost, but I find these Venture Scouts a bit earnest. Too much of this "climb every mountain, ford every stream" business. What about sloping off on our own for a bit?'

Such an honour comes the way of few Fifth formers. Gaylord cut some sandwiches, filled a Thermos with tea, packed them in his haversack, and they set off.

Awed though Gaylord was by the eminence of his companion, he could not be blind to the majesty of his surroundings.

The forest fascinated him. It was utterly different from the pastoral Trent Valley of his home: remoteness, a green mystery of firs, a glimpse of cruel, snowy peaks beyond the trees; silence; a tumbling, lonely stream; a wandering track; at night, the dancing of fireflies and, from the far forests, the sullen roar of the rutting deer. He had just emerged from the chrysalis of boyhood into the bright, perceptive world of adolescence, and

39

could scarcely believe what he saw. He began for the first time to understand a little of what chaps like Wordsworth and Keats (and even his own father) had been getting at. But surely even they hadn't seen quite this freshness of wonder? The only trouble was, this emotional reaction to nature made him feel quite old, so that suddenly he was a boy again. He took off his haversack, began to run. Roger, who, as School Captain, Captain of Rugger, and Captain of Cricket, couldn't be expected to be overawed by the majesties of mere nature, ran with him. 'Pass!' cried Gaylord, hurling the haversack to his friend. Roger caught it, ran in front, passed it back. They ran on, collapsed, panting, on the short turf beside a small lake. They undressed, swam and splashed joyfully in the lake, to the intense indignation of the waterfowl. Then, dry and dressed again, they ate their picnic sprawled on the green turf. And the boy gazed in awe at the high, sunlit peaks, and became once more a man. Joy of swift movement, joy of physical well-being, joy of solitude in nature, joy of friendship. In that moment, all these joys were Gaylord's. Joy, deep and intense.

But suddenly a chill and a shadow touched the forest. A frisson passed over the surface of the lake. Gaylord looked anxiously up at the sky. The sun had bounced against one of the high peaks, turning it to black menace. A lone bird winged home across the silent valley. 'Miles?' said Gaylord.

'What?'

'Do you know the way back?'

Roger was lying on his back, his fingers laced behind his neck. Now he lifted his head and looked at Gaylord. 'No,' he said. 'Do you?'

'No,' said Gaylord.

Suddenly Gaylord felt very low. It occurred to him that the minibus wasn't *anywhere*. It was just in one of a thousand clearings in a forest the size of Wales. So even if they met a charcoal burner, and he turned out to be an English-speaking charcoal burner, which didn't seem very likely, they didn't know where to ask him the way *to*.

Roger said lazily, 'You worry too much.'

'But it'll be dark soon,' said Gaylord.

'Well, I think its that-a-way,' said Roger. 'Come on.'

They set off. There were trees, and mountains, and tracks, just as there had been when they came. But then there were trees and mountains and tracks in every direction for hundreds of miles, thought Gaylord miserably. He would have given his most loved possession, his new boat, to see the minibus round the next bend. And the thought of proudly rowing his new boat, at home on the friendly Trent, almost made him weep. He didn't think he liked foreign parts very much.

'What's that?' Gaylord said suddenly. The menacing silence of the forest had given way to an even more menacing noise.

'It's horses,' said Roger. 'No doubt *Die Walküre* themselves.' He suddenly grabbed his young friend by the shoulders. 'Mind they don't scoop you up, young Gaylord.'

Even the fact that his idol had called him by his Christian name went almost unnoticed. The thunder of approaching hooves, in a darkling forest, was a sound too menacing and eerie for comfort.

The horse came pounding along the track. Then the rider reined it in. They saw it wasn't a horseman. It was a horsewoman. She leaned over, patting the horse's flank, and spoke to Roger in German. She did not seem to notice Gaylord.

Roger said, reluctantly, 'Over to you, Pentecost. You're doing German.'

Gaylord saw a girl, with dark, flowing hair. A gravely beautiful girl.

The only German phrase known to most Englishmen is *auf Wiedersehen*; and this, by its very nature, is not a satisfactory conversational opening. But Gaylord was able to say, with considerable aplomb, *'Enschuldigen Sie, bitte. Wir sind englisch, und wir sind gelost.'*

She looked puzzled. *'Was ist "gelost"?'* Then: 'But you say you are English. Why do you not *speak* English?'

'We thought you were German.'

'I am. But I learned English at school. We all do.'

'I say. You speak it jolly well,' said Roger, who believed that foreigners always needed putting at their ease, even on their own ground.

'But of course,' said the girl.

'We're lost,' said Gaylord, getting down to business.

'Lost? Why, where do you want to go?'

'We don't know,' Gaylord said miserably.

'Then that makes it difficult to direct you,' the girl said severely. She turned to Roger. 'Do you know anyone in England who wants an au pair girl?'

'Yes. My mother,' Gaylord said.

'So!' She slapped the horse's neck. The horse quivered, and stamped his foot. 'She does? My mother will let me go only on personal recommendation.'

'I can personally recommend my mother,' Gaylord said eagerly.

'That is what one would expect,' said the girl.

'You've got a smashing horse,' said Roger, beginning to feel left out. But the girl ignored him, and concentrated on Gaylord. 'Is your mother of the English aristocracy?' she asked.

'I'm afraid not.' He looked crestfallen.

'Never mind. It is not essential. But you

must come up to the house, and meet my mother, and explain to her. Does your mother want someone at once?'

'Yes.'

'I am Christine Haldt. I will walk with you.' She jumped down from her horse, took the bridle. She was nearly as tall as Roger and Gaylord. She wore a black jacket and riding breeches. She tossed her hair out of her eyes, turned and gave Roger an appraising look. 'Prince von Bismarck was once in love with my great-grandmama,' she said.

'Really?'

'It is not far to the castle,' she said.

'I suppose – you don't happen to have seen a minibus around?' Gaylord asked anxiously.

She ignored him. 'But great-grandmama threw an apfel strudel at him,' she informed Roger. For the first time she laughed. 'Was not that harum-scarum?'

CHAPTER 4

And now Christine Haldt was no longer in the Bavarian forests. She was standing on the Pentecost doorstep, warmly shaking hands with a tall English woman who, quite frankly, was not wholeheartedly reciprocating the warmth.

'Do come inside,' said May, who felt that there was quite a bit of groundwork to be cleared before they got on to Onkel Willi.

'Thank you.' The girl came into the hall, dumped a suitcase and a haversack. Then: 'Excuse,' she said, went outside and came back with skis, ski sticks, and ski boots.

'God bless my soul,' said May. 'You can't ski in England.'

'No. Not in the Trent valley, in August. I know.' She laughed gaily. 'But Aviemore is not bad.'

'But Aviemore's miles away.'

'Of course. It is in Scotland. Are you acquainted with the poet Burns?'

'Not personally,' said May.

'That I understand. He is long dead.'

'I'm sorry,' said May, contrite. 'We English can never resist a temptation to be flippant.' She motioned to the girl to sit down. 'If you had been staying, Miss Haldt, it is something you would have had to learn to put up with. But I am afraid you cannot stay. It was very, very wrong of my son to tell you I wanted an au pair girl. I don't.'

Christine looked at her with great severity. 'You are sending me away? I do not please you?'

'You please me very much. I just don't want an au pair girl.'

'Perhaps you think I will seduce your son.

That is not so. I am virtuous. Besides, he is too young.'

May was stung. 'Why, how old are you?'

'Seventeen.'

'Well, Gaylord's nearly seventeen.'

'Maybe. But a child, an infant.'

May burned to say: if you got to know him better, you would soon learn that he's very wise and mature for his age. But she wasn't going to be pushed into a proud mother act. She said, 'Of course, we shall pay your return fare, and make all arrangements for your journey, and apologize most deeply for the inconvenience we have caused you. Though–' she smiled – 'frankly, my dear, you did rather jump the gun, didn't you?'

'Gun?' Christine wrinkled her lovely brow. 'I do not understand jumping the gun.'

'No. It's an English idiom. You might even say slang.'

'And what is this jumping the gun? A sport, yes?'

May nodded. She was beginning to feel exhausted.

But Christine was intrigued. Preparatory to her visit she had made a special study of English sports. But jumping the gun she had not come across. She must ask Gaylord, she told herself.

May said, 'And of course you are welcome to stay for a night or two. We wouldn't be so churlish as to send you straight back.'

'That is good.' She gave May a charming, sudden smile. 'It will give me time to inveigle myself into all your hearts, so that you will not send me away.' And for the first time she took off her sunglasses; and May found herself looking into a pair of brown eyes as fine and beautiful as her own grey ones.

May glanced at her watch. 'We usually meet in the living room for a glass of sherry about seven. So if I show you your room now it will give you time to bath and change, and then I'll call for you and take you down to meet the family. I thought,' she added, 'it might be easier for you that way.'

The girl bowed. 'You are kind and thoughtful, Mrs Pentecost. I do not allow myself to appear shy, but shyness is nevertheless one of my failings. Is the family large?'

'No. There's Gaylord's grandfather. Actually, it's his house, though he doesn't work the farm any more. He's a bit fierce-looking, but really he wouldn't hurt a fly.'

'At home, the Grandfather is also fierce, but then it is also his house. He says to the Father "do this, so." And to my mother, "let this be done".'

May was intrigued. 'And do they do it?'

'But *naturlich*. He is the Grandfather.'

'Yes; well, it's a bit different here,' said May, trying to imagine herself taking orders from her father-in-law. 'Grandpa's very fierce, but no one takes a great deal of notice.'

'Then what is the point of being fierce?'

It was a good question; but not one May felt like tackling at the moment. She said, 'Then there is my husband. I think you'll like him. He's an author.'

'An author!' The girl clapped her hands. 'But why did your son not tell me?'

'I don't suppose it occurred to him.'

'But an author – that is wonderful.'

'It's a living,' said May. 'Just.' She always kept a small fire extinguisher handy for any young woman who might see her husband as a combination of Count Tolstoy, Balzac, and Dostoyevsky. Jocelyn soaked up adulation as a sponge soaks up water.

'In Germany,' said Christine, 'we treat authors with the respect we show to all creative artists.'

'In England,' said May, 'they're often young men trying to make a scraggy beard and a sparse talent go further than nature ever intended.'

The girl smiled. 'I am sure that does not describe your husband.'

'It certainly doesn't. Jocelyn has plenty of talent. And no beard.' May smiled back. 'Then there are my children. Gaylord you've met. Amanda is ten, and worldly-wise.' And breathtakingly innocent, she added to herself. 'That's all. Now.' She rose. 'I will show you your room.'

CHAPTER 5

Between six and seven o'clock, a number of people prepared to move towards their objective: the large, casually comfortable living room of the Pentecosts.

Old John Pentecost was already there, reading *The Times*, in so far as anyone *could* be said to be reading *The Times* when Amanda was in the same room. 'Did you have a nice holiday at your Club, Grandpa?'

'It wasn't a holiday. I was simply put out to grass while your parents went gadding off to Welsh Wales.'

'Are the members all old?'

He rattled his paper irritably. 'They're not old at all. One or two of them are younger than me, even.'

She looked unimpressed. 'Had a lot died since last year?' she asked sympathetically.

They had, frankly. But he wasn't admitting it. 'You morbid little creature. Of course not.'

'I bet they had. Teacher says death is the last great taboo. She says people don't talk about it any more. So I bet lots and lots of them died, but they wouldn't tell you.'

'Tcha!' said Grandpa, trying to concentrate

on a leader about Ireland. But it was no use. Time's Wingéd Chariot was making such a commotion he couldn't hear himself think.

Charles Bunting said, 'Let's drop in and have some sherry with the Pentecosts. I want to pin May down about that portrait.'

Liz tried to hide her elation. Gaylord should be home from Germany by now. She had thought up a hundred reasons for going to The Cypresses, and abandoned them all. (Since her father had discovered her guilty secret, she had tried harder than ever to hide it from others.) But here was Father handing her a reason on a plate. She jumped at it.

Gaylord came in from painting his boat. Amanda said, 'I think it was foul of you not to come to Wales, Gaylord. Don't you think it was foul of Gaylord not to come to Wales, Grandpa?'

'Don't see why. You'd got your parents. And young What's-her-name Bunting.'

'Yes. But the parents are a bit stricken in years, aren't they?'

'One foot in the grave, both of them,' Grandpa said sourly. He hadn't read the business pages yet. But he supposed he ought to have a friendly word with young Gaylord. He had a strong sense of duty, and he hadn't seen the lad since he got back. He lowered his paper, gave his grandson a tigerish grin. 'Well, learnt your lesson? Thankful to be back in England? Not going

50

abroad again, I'll wager.'

Gaylord was still feeling deflated. 'I take it *you* don't think an au pair girl's a good idea, either?'

'I think it's a damned awful idea. I'm not having any young foreign females in *my* house. It'll be either Bach's Organ Fugues all day, or pop.' (For Grandpa, music meant either Sousa's Marches, or the less demanding bits of Gilbert and Sullivan. Anything outside this somewhat limited range was anathema to the old man.)

Amanda said, 'Joan Carpenter's parents had a Spanish one and she played a guitar all day and sang sad Basque folk songs a tone flat.'

Grandpa shuddered, a fact noted by Amanda, who missed very little. She said, 'Joan said it sent her grandfather into a decline. In the end he begged to be allowed to go into an Eventide Home.'

'What's all this about?' asked Jocelyn, wandering in at this moment.

Gaylord said, 'Mother said she wanted an au pair. And I arranged for one to come from Germany. And now Mother's changed her mind.' He looked anxiously but not hopefully at his father. Gaylord never expected Father to *do* anything. But it was pleasant to have him to talk to occasionally. You never felt he was more than half listening, so you didn't have a conscience if you went on a bit.

There was a cheerful tap at the door. 'Come in,' called Grandpa. Charles Bunting came in with Liz. 'Hi, young Liz,' said Gaylord. 'Join me in a sherry.' He filled two glasses, carried them across. He thought young Liz looked rather super. He was suddenly aware of the fact, for the first time, that she was no longer a child of eleven, but a girl of seventeen. And it was beginning to dawn on him that girls of seventeen were not just inferior chaps. They were rather interesting creatures in their own right.

Liz took her sherry reverently from his hands. She smiled at him happily. He'd come home, safe! And they were still on holiday. She said, 'Did you have a good time in Germany?'

'Yes, thank you. What about Wales?'

'Lovely. Your parents were sweet to me.' They clinked glasses, smiled. He'd never been so friendly. She really felt he was seeing her with new eyes. I'm sure, she thought pathetically, desperately, he's beginning to see me as something more than young Liz.

May came in, with Christine.

Christine had changed into fresh denims, and looked stunning. Grandpa heaved himself to his feet again, bowed courteously. Didn't know who she might be, but it was always nice to have a pretty girl about the place. Charles and Jocelyn were already on their feet. May said, 'My father-in-law, John Pentecost. My husband. Mr Bunting and Liz. Gaylord you know. Amanda.' Then she said, 'This is Fräulein Christine Haldt, who is visiting us for a day or two.'

Poor Liz! On the Roller Coaster of her love life she was used to sudden descents. But this was the most sudden descent of all. Gaylord *must* have brought her back from Germany! There was no other possible explanation. And as for Amanda, she was livid. There was only one thought in her mind: to get this girl back to Germany. But how? She hadn't much faith in witchcraft, and at the moment she couldn't think of anything else.

There was a chorus of how-do-you-do's. But to Gaylord the girl held out a hand, palm downward. And Gaylord, to his mother's utter astonishment, and to Liz's despair, and Amanda's fury, stepped forward, took the girl's hand, bowed over it, brushed it with his lips, and murmured, *'Gnädiges* Fräulein! How on earth did YOU get here?' Then he said firmly, 'What do you mean, Mother? A day or two? If Christine's come all this way to be our au pair girl, you can't send her back now.' He sought reinforcements, and knew it was no use asking Father, much as he liked him. 'Can she, Grandfather?'

The old man said, 'Well, at least the young

lady can stay as our guest while we think it over. Come and sit by me, my dear.' He paused beside his own chair. 'Now, Miss er–? What can I get you to drink?'

'Oh, anything, please. Champagne, Coke, it does not matter.'

He poured her a sherry, sank into his chair. 'Now, what is it? Christine? That is a beautiful name. In England, of course, we say Christeen,' he added with a touch of reproof.

Christine gave him a devastating smile. He called out, 'You know, May, we must think about this very carefully. You *could* do with some help. You've been looking a bit peaky lately, I've often thought.'

'Rubbish!' muttered Amanda, sticking her lower lip out. Fortunately for her, no one heard her.

'You really have, old girl,' said Jocelyn, looking at this blooming Rhine Maiden, then at his wife.

'*You'd* like her to stay, wouldn't you, Daddy?' cooed Amanda sweetly, speaking to her father but watching her mother.

May felt suddenly old. And even older when Gaylord, springing to her defence, said, 'Oh, I don't know. You can't expect Mum to look like a seventeen-year-old. *I* don't think she's too decrepit for her age.'

'Thank you, darling,' May said gratefully. Then she turned back to her father-in-law. 'I can manage perfectly well,' she said quietly but forcibly.

''Course she can,' muttered Amanda.

'Still think you'd do with some help, May,' the old man said, looking appreciatively at Christine.

'After all, we *can* afford it, old girl,' said Jocelyn.

May said, 'Has *either* of you been neglected in any way?'

'Good lord, no,' said Jocelyn.

'Only thinking of you, May,' said Grandpa, hurt. Touchy creatures, women!

'Then I suggest you leave me to run things in my own way, both of you.'

'Hear, jolly hear,' cried Amanda. 'Good old Mum! You can do your own sludge-bumping, can't you, Mum.'

'Be *quiet*, Amanda,' said May.

Christine addressed May. 'What, please, is this sludge-bumping of which the child speaks?'

Amanda said, 'The child's name is Amanda. Her friends called her Mandy.' She did not sound as though she thought Christine would ever get to the Mandy stage.

May said, 'Sludge-bumping means scrubbing floors. But it is a word used only by ill-mannered little creatures like my daughter.' She gave Amanda a look.

Gaylord said to Christine, 'Come and meet Liz.' He led her across. 'This is Liz Bunting. We played together as kids. Didn't we, Liz?'

'That's right,' said Liz, unable to think of anything more sparkling.

Christine said, 'I too had a childhood friend of the opposite sex, Otto Muller. We skied, and went mountain climbing, and skated, and wandered in the great forests. What did you do?' she asked Liz.

Liz said, 'We had a contraption: a couple of planks on wheels, and we used to ride on that. And – and we had bicycles, and–' She petered out.

'What fun!' said Christine, without enthusiasm.

'And we paddled in the river,' said Liz, suddenly inspired.

Christine was silent. Then she said, 'But Otto grew very tiresome. A playmate of my childhood, I tell you, and suddenly he is wishing to seduce me. I think it is very foolish to fall in love with a childhood playmate,' she added sternly.

'Very,' said Gaylord.

'Very,' said Liz in a small voice.

'Shall we go in to supper?' said May.

'Now, May. When am I going to start this portrait?' said Charles who, with Liz, had been invited to stay and take potluck.

May said, 'Charles, you're not still on with that?'

'Oh, don't be so damned coy. I'll be

around tomorrow afternoon. You can spare me an hour, you know you can.'

'Please, May,' said Jocelyn.

'Oh, all right. Thank you, Charles. I know it's an honour. It's just – well, who am I, to be painted in oils?'

'You're May Pentecost,' Jocelyn said simply.

'With a rather interesting bone structure,' said Charles.

'Not at all a bad sort of Mum, as Mums go,' said Gaylord.

'And a damned fine woman,' said Grandpa, lifting his glass. May was terribly touched. These tributes had been too sudden, too unexpected. Her voice shook as she said, 'Thank you, gentlemen. After that, to refuse would be churlish. You and Liz come to lunch, Charles.'

Christine said, 'I will look after the house and its inmates while you sit for your portrait, Frau Pentecost. In doing so I shall make myself indispensable, and you will not then cruelly send me away.' She smiled charmingly.

Amanda amused herself by staring at Christine and letting the tiniest sliver of tongue appear between her lips. No one, not even Mummy, could accuse her of putting her tongue out. But *she* knew what she was doing. It gave her immense satisfaction.

But grandpa looked uneasy. 'I'm not living

57

on sauerkraut and sausage, young woman.'

'You will not have to, sir. Not for nothing have I taken examinations in haute cuisine. English cooking will be–'

'A piece of cake?' suggested Gaylord.

She looked at him with interest. 'What is that? Another English idiom? Or do you really think I will serve the Grandfather cake for breakfast?' she asked scornfully, but giving the Grandfather an encouraging smile. Then she turned her attention to Jocelyn. 'Sir, Frau Pentecost tells me you are an author. I should think it an inestimable honour if I might help in some humble way – typing, reading proofs, all those menial tasks that must come between you and your wonderful inspiration.'

'Daddy *will* like that, won't you, Daddy?' Amanda said enthusiastically.

Jocelyn looked both touched and flattered, and thanked Christine very charmingly. But May, who did all the typing and filing, and had never thought of it as being either humble or menial, bridled. A vision of that beautiful head bowed over *her* typewriter, while Jocelyn's inspiration soared – a vision suggested by Christine and cunningly underlined by Amanda – did not appeal. Where Jocelyn was concerned, she was possessive, she admitted it. But then, Jocelyn was worth being possessive about. And Jocelyn was a man. And May worked on the simple assumption that to trust *any* man, even Jocelyn, with a beautiful seventeen-year-old was asking for trouble. Besides, she was still remembering the astonishing sight of her English son kissing a woman's hand, and so obviously enjoying it.

Gaylord, too, was remembering it. Christine's hand had been delightfully soft and cool. And as he touched it with his lips he smelt the most delicate and lovely fragrance. The softness, the fragrance, was something from a new world, from a world of hitherto unimagined excitements and delights. He said, 'It would be a super arrangement if Christine could stay, Mum.' It would, too. It seemed to him it would help everybody – his mother, Father, Christine. It might even – though this of course was the least important – it might even be nice for himself to have her around.

The grandfather clock in the hall struck ten. John Pentecost yawned, snapped open his hunter and said, 'Well, I don't know about you lot, but I'm ready for bed.' Just as he did every night when the grandfather clock struck ten.

To Christine's astonishment no one took the slightest notice. At home, everyone would have been crowding through the door by now, at such a hint from the Grandfather. She jumped nervously to her feet. May said,

'Are you tired, dear? You must be, after all that travelling. Good night. I'll bring you a cup of tea when it's time to get up.'

'Tea? In my room? Before I am up?'

'Of course.'

'Where do I drink it?'

'In bed, usually,' May said smiling.

Christine looked at May. Then she grinned knowingly. 'Now it is I who will use the English idiom, Mrs Pentecost. Pull the other one. It has bells upon it.'

May, for once, looked lost. Gaylord said, 'They don't have morning tea in Germany, Mum.'

'Good God,' said Grandpa. He'd always known there was something damned un-English about foreigners.

Jocelyn said, 'But you can't regain consciousness without a cup of tea. It's – the kiss of life.'

Christine said, 'So. You sleep. Someone comes into your room with a cup of tea. Even when you are not ill. The cock crows. You wake, drink the horrible tea, *in bed*, then you dress?'

'The life-giving tea,' Jocelyn corrected devoutly.

Christine tried to imagine it. The natives certainly had some very strange customs.

Charles Bunting drove Liz home in silence. Slowly and thoughtfully, seldom touching even sixty. Tomorrow, he was going to begin a work that excited him more than anything he had done for a long time. Since he could not have the flesh and blood woman, he would re-create her for himself. Pygmalion in reverse.

Already, in the privacy of his studio, he'd done a number of sketches. But tomorrow he would start on the real thing: the creation of a canvas that would show not only the beauty of lips and cheek and eyes, but also the soul and spirit of a woman of noble character. Will it also, he wondered, show my love; and dismissed the thought as sentimental, unworthy of a true artist. No, this picture would show May Pentecost in every facet of her personality. It would also contain every grain of art and skill and craft of which Charles Bunting was capable. He owed that to May. She would be his masterpiece: *Portrait of an Unknown Woman. By Charles Bunting*, distant generations would read in their catalogues. When he, and she, and Jocelyn were dust, his signature and her face, forever linked, would be stared at by the grandchildren of men and women yet unborn.

He would show her as she was: no longer a girl; a woman, a wife and mother, still beautiful, at rest beside the fire. He would show her serenity, her humour, her strength. He would give May Pentecost that gift which only an artist can bestow: her immortality.

At rest beside the fire ... what was that thing of Ronsard's? *Assise auprès du feu, dévidant et filant Direz... Ronsard me célébrait du temps que j'étais belle.*

How had old Ronsard finished? *Vivez, n'attendez à demain: Cueillez dès aujourd'hui les roses de la vie.*

Well, it was no use expecting May to gather any roses with him. May had gathered the roses of *her* life with a good and kind man, with an ordered way of life and fine children. But what about himself? What roses had *he* gathered since Rachel died? Wealth. Fame. But, for the rest, he had given: given himself, his time, his thoughts, his feelings, a living sacrifice to his work. If he was now one of the most acclaimed artists in Britain, it was because he had spurned the toys that pleased other men. He had – a daughter he loved. Was it not time now to gather the roses of *his* life, before the time came when the petals must fall at the touch of his fingers?

It was. But not with May, not with Jocelyn's wife. Lord, he thought, not for the first time. What a handicap a puritan upbringing is to a man!

Tomorrow! Tomorrow he would learn how well his hand could portray the picture that was already in his mind. And he hadn't much doubt. He had taught his hands, over the years, skills to interpret his mind. In fact, he had only one doubt: the sitter. He needed her serious co-operation. And he wasn't sure he would get it. May had an unpredictable streak of flippancy (the Whistler's Mother remark was a case in point), and if she insisted on treating the sitting as a bit of a lark, he'd get furious and that would ruin everything. Worse. He knew that whatever role May was playing, she always remained wife and mother first. And if she was up and down like a yo-yo, looking after her family, he'd probably finish by smashing his canvas over his knee.

Liz welcomed her father's silence. She burrowed into the deep leather of the Rolls, and gave herself up to misery.

She tried to recapture the scene when Gaylord brought her a sherry. 'Hi, young Liz, join me in a sherry.' And he had looked at her. Surprised. Admiring. *Good Lord*, he had thought, *young Liz has grown up. Into a beautiful and attractive woman. Why didn't I see it before? I must have been blind. Well, from now on–* And then the door had opened. And a minute later Gaylord, poised and elegant, had been bowing over a German woman's hand. And soon he had been agreeing that to fall in love with a childhood playmate was foolish in the extreme. Oh, what a fool she'd been, to imagine all that nonsense about herself going through his mind. If he'd been interested in her at all this evening, it was

63

probably to compare home product unfavourably with the continental model.

And they were invited to lunch tomorrow! She wouldn't go, she'd find some excuse. For one of Gaylord's oldest friends to play second fiddle to someone he'd brought back from abroad would be too humiliating. (Cigars for Father, a cuckoo clock for Amanda, and an au pair for Mother and himself, that was about the size of it.) For once in her life, the gentle Liz was verging on the bloody-minded.

CHAPTER 6

May's scalp prickled. She dug her husband in the ribs. 'Jocelyn, wake up. There's someone in the house. I've heard them for some time.'

'Where?'

'Downstairs. I think they're methodically stripping the place.'

Jocelyn liked to get all his facts in place before he committed himself to action, if any. Now he said, 'Sure you didn't dream it, old girl?'

'Of *course* I didn't dream it.' She listened. 'One of them's coming up on the landing,' she whispered, on the verge of panic.

Jocelyn looked at his watch. Just gone six,

and chinks of daylight through the heavy curtains. 'They must be on overtime,' he said.

There was a knock at the door. May clung to Jocelyn. Jocelyn switched the light on. 'No,' whispered May. 'We're safer in the dark.' Too late. The door opened. Fräulein Christine Haldt appeared. She was carrying a tray containing a teapot and two glasses, and showing what May felt to be a more than adequate amount of bosom. 'Good morning,' she said brightly. 'See! I grow accustomed to your English ways. Now I pour out your life-giving tea, Herr Pentecost.'

'Thanks! Thanks awfully,' said Jocelyn.

May said, 'We don't usually have it quite so early, Christine.'

'No? Then I take it back, and bring it again in half an hour.' She picked up the tray. 'Gaylord also said it was the middle of the night, but I thought he made an English joke.'

May said, 'You've already taken Gaylord some tea?' Instinctively she pulled the neck of her own nightdress across. The girl saw the gesture, interpreted it correctly. 'My chest? It offends you?'

'It doesn't offend *me*, dear.' May was annoyed with herself for what must seem a prudish gesture. 'You look very nice. It's just that, if you're taking tea to Gaylord's grandfather – well he's a bit old-fashioned–'

'You do not think I behave like a loose

woman? That is not indeed my intention, Mrs Pentecost.'

'My dear Miss Haldt! Of *course* I don't think anything of the kind.'

'It is said my Aunt Ulrike was not averse to a little slap and tickle.' She looked suddenly anxious. 'I use the idiom correctly?'

'Yes. Though–'

'But only with those of birth and position, I need hardly say. For myself, however, I am not like that. It would not be in accordance with my nature.'

'I'm sure it wouldn't, my dear.'

'Do give me that tray,' said Jocelyn.

She gave it him. 'Alas! I could find no lemon. Now I go and make myself seemly to take tea to the Grandfather.' She reached the door.

May said, 'I think I should leave the old gentleman's tea until eight o'clock, Christine. He might not appreciate–'

'So I take it at eight.' But she was still worried. She turned back. '*You* do not think I behave like a loose woman, Herr Pentecost?'

'Good heavens, no,' said Jocelyn, looking dejectedly at a glass of sugarless, milkless tea in which floated innumerable tea leaves. 'She didn't let the water boil,' he said as the door closed behind her.

'What time is it?' May said wearily.

'Ten past six.'

66

They sipped in silence. There was a knock on the door. 'Come in,' said Jocelyn, watching the door with an eagerness May was, for once, too sleepy to notice.

Christine came in. She was wearing a roll neck skiing jumper, and a skiing scarf. Jocelyn hid his disappointment. 'I cover my chest,' she said. 'It is better?'

'*I* think so, dear. For mornings. The other would have been splendid for a rather grand ball. But–'

'Thank you. I wish always to observe the proprieties. And now if you wish, I will run your baths for you, Mr and Mrs Pentecost. Fifty-five Celsius, or do you like cold?'

May said, 'Look, Miss Haldt, we don't usually get up quite so early. Wouldn't you like to go back to bed until about eight, and be down for breakfast at 8.30?'

'What's Celsius?' said Jocelyn.

'Maybe I go back to bed, maybe not. Maybe I vacuum the carpets.' She gave May the sweetest of smiles.

She went. May flung herself back on her pillow with a groan. But Jocelyn was still sitting up in bed looking worried. 'What is Celsius?'

'I think it's what we call Centigrade.'

'Good Lord.' He looked at her with admiration. 'Thought it must be something like Badedas.'

May said, 'For heaven's sake lie down and

snatch a little sleep, man. If that girl starts vacuuming at 6.30 in the morning, your father will rouse the entire household in his fury.'

The door opened. May jerked up as though the electric blanket had suddenly become live. But it was only Gaylord. 'Hello, Mum. Mind if I take the boat out?'

'*Now*? My dear boy, do you know what time it is?'

'Six fifteen. It's a super morning. The hillside's dew-pearled, all that sort of thing.'

'You will be careful?' May would have felt much happier if he'd gone later, when there would be people around to fish him out if he fell in. But she never pandered to motherly fears. 'Try to avoid the weir.'

'Do my best.' He grinned, kissed her forehead. 'So long. So long, Dad.'

Jocelyn raised a weary head. 'Did *you* know Celsius was German for Centigrade?'

''Course. Back for breakfast.' He went downstairs. Christine was in the kitchen, lugging the vacuum cleaner out of a cupboard. She smiled, friendly. 'You want breakfast?'

'No, thanks. Going out.' He felt he ought to say, 'Come with me,' but he didn't want a bally girl destroying the peace of this morning with her chatter. Then he realized that Christine was dressed more for the nursery slopes than for an English kitchen. 'Off skiing, old girl?'

She looked at him coldly. 'That is an English joke?'

'Yes. Sorry, Christine.'

She understood. 'Mr Pentecost wishes me to appear seemly when I take the Grandfather his tea.'

'Oh. Ah. Yes,' said Gaylord. Now he came to think of it, it occurred to him that Christine had looked all right before. Very fetching, in fact. And you couldn't expect a man of Grandpa's age to notice things like that. He sighed. Mum could be a bit of a fusspot, at times. Still– 'So long,' he said. And went out into the bright morning.

He went through the stack yard, across the diamond-strewn paddock. In the orchard the apples glowed round and plump in the level rays. He strode through the high, wet grass. He sniffed the harsh smell of grass and nettles, then the smell of the river was dank in his nostrils. He came to the sweep of the river, to the landing stage where his boat was moored.

He jumped into the boat, cast off, settled the oars into the rowlocks, pulled vigorously away. Upstream, that's where the joy was, to pull against the swirling waters, to conquer by strength of arm and thigh, to watch the bank and the hedges and the trees creep slowly by at his will, while the timbers creaked in protest, and the little waves slapped ineffectually at the bows. Then, panting, physically stretched, to lie back in the drifting boat, to smell the river smell, to feel the sun already on cheek and thigh, to hear the gurgling of the stream and the lowing of cattle, to dip a hand into the moving stream, to see – the depth of blue heaven, the little, distant hills, the trees, the dancing water. To have his senses so exquisitely pampered, while the mind went its own journeys; there was just a possibility he'd be tried for the First XV next term – running up on the wing, a second fleeter than your opponents, the urgent thud of boots on turf, the smack of leather, the smell of mud and sweat and trampled grass...

The boat was broadside on in a backwater. Lazily he picked up an oar, and leaning on one elbow brought the boat round to drift back with the stream. Other journeys: cycling home from school on that last day of term, to a family strewn carelessly about the orchard: Dad, Grandpa, young Amanda who wasn't bad as kid sisters went, Mum: Mum who, though he would never have admitted it to a soul, and least of all to her, was quite bearable. He smiled, remembering that there had been a period in his youth when he'd actually wanted to marry her, until he found there were certain difficulties. Oh, and young Liz and her father. Young Liz was all right. Bit drippy, but then girls were.

The boat drifted on, a little faster now as

the river felt the pull of the distant weir. And a thought suddenly struck him: Christine wasn't drippy. Christine's hands were soft and fragrant; Christine, bringing his morning tea, had made him feel, for the first time in his life, shy and awkward; Christine in the kitchen had looked capable and friendly and jolly attractive. He wondered now why he hadn't brought her along. But then he thought: if I'd brought Liz with me this morning, she'd have insisted on my resting in the stern while she did the rowing. If I'd brought Christine she'd have sat in the stern and told me what I was doing wrong with my oars. No. A chap was better on his own. A girl was only a girl, however interesting she might look in a blue négligé.

The stream was moving quite quickly now. And there was the landing stage. He sat up, set the oars in the rowlocks, pulled strongly across to the shore. He tied up the boat; and ran joyously home to breakfast; meeting, on the way, his friend Roger Miles who had just been for a swim.

Roger looked very handsome, black hair wet, and sleek, his chiselled features given an even sharper chiselling by exercise and cold water. 'Hello, young Pentecost,' he said loftily.

'Hello, Miles,' said Gaylord. (In Germany, in a foreign land, they had become for a time Roger and Gaylord. But now, back in

England, Roger was making it quite clear that protocol would be observed.) 'I say, you remember that girl we met in Germany?'

'Which one?' asked Miles, who had met several.

'Christine Haldt.'

'The one at the Slosh? *Very* nice. What about her?'

'She's turned up.'

'Turned up where?'

'At home. To be Mother's au pair. Except that Mother doesn't seem to want an au pair,' he added gloomily.

'Good Lord. You mean – she's actually in England? Here?'

'Yes.' Gaylord was flattered to have made such an impression on this near-deity.

They walked on. 'This towel's damnably wet and cold,' said Miles.

'I'll have it,' said Gaylord.

Miles gave it him. 'You doing anything this morning?' he suddenly asked.

'No. Nothing at all, Miles.'

'I'll come over, later. If I'm not too busy. We might have a knock-up, or something.'

Gaylord could scarcely believe his ears. Roger Miles, Captain of Cricket, actually suggesting a knock-up with someone who wasn't even in the *XV!* And not summoning Gaylord to *his* place, but humbly offering to come to Gaylord's! Gaylord was no longer wading in wet grass. He was walking on air.

They came to where their ways parted. Gaylord made to hand back the towel. Miles said, 'I wonder if you'd stick it on a line for me, and I'll collect it when I come. I hate wet towels.' He gave Gaylord his quick-as-a-flash smile.

'Of course, Miles.' It would be an honour.

'So long,' said Miles. He turned away. 'Funny about that girl, isn't it?'

Jocelyn was soon asleep again. But May was wide awake, thoughts churning round in her head like clothes in a washing machine: the disturbing, yet undoubtedly warm, feeling that old Charles was in love with her, and that this afternoon she was to sit for him, and that – good portraitist that he was – he was going to look deep into her soul and put down what he saw. She thought of Christine, so young and fresh and feminine in the early morning; of Gaylord, her indemonstrably loved son; sweet Amanda, and sad, loving Liz. All of them innocent and fresh as the morning, while she – oh, what weariness and doubts lay hidden in the heart of a woman of forty!

In this room, the morning was a few streaks of brilliance between the curtains. Out there it was dancing water, swallow flight, lark song, joy, all nature saying simply and easily what Schiller and Beethoven had striven so nobly to say. And in the centre of it, Gaylord her son, between sparkling waves and blue heaven, careless days of holiday still before him; all life, the pain and sweetness of love, the joy of struggle and achievement, the quiet joys of everyday things – all these before him. No. She wasn't envious. May Pentecost envied no one. She just wished she could be – for an hour, for this bright morning – seventeen once more.

There was sudden uproar – from downstairs an angry roaring and howling, interspersed with bumps. Jocelyn lifted his head an inch from the pillow. 'Wha's that?

'Miss Haldt hoovering.'

He sank back. 'Thought it was Concorde.' He was asleep again.

But May was even more awake than before. She sat, hugging her knees. 'Wait for it,' she told herself gleefully.

She did not have to wait long. She heard a door being wrenched open on the landing, the hurried shuffle of slippers down the stairs, the huffing and puffing and angry muttering of a grandfather roused unceremoniously at six-thirty in the morning. 'Darling,' she murmured to her sleeping spouse, 'it looks like another threat to Anglo-German relations.' She got no reply. Sighing, she lay down and, to her surprise, found herself drifting into sleep.

The old man flung open the living-room

74

door. 'May, what the blazes do you think–? Oh, sorry. Didn't know it was you, Frawleen.' (Grandpa never pandered to foreigners' peculiar views on how to pronounce their own languages.)

Christine, for once in her life, looked startled. To anger the Grandfather must surely be the quickest way possible to get sent back home. She said, 'You do not wish me to vacuum?'

Grandpa saw the startled look, was immediately contrite. 'My dear young lady, it's just that – at my age – one sleeps so little, and – when one *has* managed to drop off–' said Grandpa, who invariably slept solidly from the moment his head touched the pillow to the moment Jocelyn walked in with his morning tea.

Christine said, 'I am about to bring you tea. But Mrs Pentecost says it is too early. So – I vacuum.'

'Quite right, my dear. Very helpful.'

'Also, for you, I cover my chest.' She pointed to her sweater. 'You find me seemly, *nicht wahr?*'

'Very seemly,' said Grandpa, who wasn't used to having the conversation taken out of his hands in this way.

'At home the Grandfather takes much interest in the deer feeding, hunting, shooting. Here you have no deer?' she asked sympathetically.

'Afraid not,' said Grandpa, feeling deprived.

'It is good for you to have deer, many deer. Then you go out hunting, crawling all day on your belly on the mountainside. Then at night you sleep.' She laughed gaily. 'So. It does not matter to you that the au pair vacuums at dawn.'

'You're not the au pair,' Grandpa pointed out. You didn't catch John Pentecost like that.

Her face fell. 'But you are the Grandfather. If you say "This Christine must stay," then I stay. The Grandfather's word is like the Word of God.'

'My dear child, you don't know Mrs Pentecost. She is a dashed fine woman, but you don't try coming the Word of God with her. Besides–' He looked uncomfortable. But he was always honest – 'I don't think I want an au pair in the house either.'

'No? Even if I do not reveal my bosom, or bring your tea before eight o'clock, or vacuum before nine?'

'Even then.'

She was silent, hanging her head. Then, without looking at him again, she went from the room, stumped miserably upstairs, threw her things into her cases, collected her skis, ski sticks and ski boots, and went to see Mrs Pentecost.

May was wakened by the clatter of skis and

ski sticks on the landing. She switched on the light. 7.10. She looked to see where the noise was coming from.

Christine stood in the doorway, forlorn. Her ski boots hung round her neck. She carried a suitcase and a haversack. May said, 'Christine, my dear! What's the matter?'

'The Grandfather bids me be gone,' said Christine.

'Nonsense. I never heard of such a thing. You're our guest – for a night or two,' she finished cautiously.

'But one cannot gainsay the Grandfather.'

'One can certainly gainsay the Grandfather. I spend most of my life doing it. Now you go and unpack your things again and I'll speak to Mr Pentecost.'

But the girl did not move. She said, 'I make the tea too early, and I hear Mr Pentecost say I do not boil the kettle. I am immodest in my dress. I exacerbate the Grandfather's insomnia with my too early vacuuming. So now he says: "I do not wish an au pair. Frau Pentecost does not wish an au pair. Be gone!"' She burst into tears. 'So I go,' she wailed.

'Oh, Lord,' said May. A sudden, warm affection brought her out of bed to throw her arms round the unhappy girl. 'Now Christine, you've misunderstood the old gentleman. He is the kindest of men. He – I – we shall all be delighted to have you for a

77

few days.'

'But not as your au pair,' Christine sniffed accusingly.

'Well, we shall have to see about that. You see, I imagine there are all sorts of things – work permits, agreements – it would have to be gone into.'

Christine shook her head. 'I go now. It is better. It is but a few kilometres walk to the station. Eventually there will come a train, even in England. It is better so.'

Gaylord barged in, and was intrigued to find his mother in her nightie embracing a Christine departing apparently for the slopes. He looked at them, shook his head. 'I just can't imagine,' he said.

'Your grandfather's upset Christine,' said May. 'She says she is going.'

'Oh, *don't* go,' said Gaylord. 'Roger Miles is coming round for a spot of cricket later. I'd thought he might be interested to see you again.'

'Roger Miles? He whom I met in Bavaria?'

'That's right. The chap I said was School Captain,' Gaylord said devoutly.

Christine turned to May. 'Mrs Pentecost, if you – if both of us – begged the Grandfather to let me stay, he would, you really believe, relent?'

'Just you leave him to me,' said May. 'But only for a day or two, mind.'

Christine gave her a delighted smile. But

she was astonished. It seemed to her that English women took far too many liberties with their menfolk.

Jocelyn said sleepily, 'I dreamed you were talking to someone.'

May said, 'That was no dream, brother. I've been fighting a rearguard action.' She pondered. 'Jocelyn, would you say I was pretty immovable, once I'd made my mind up?'

'I would say more. I would say that you and the rock of Gibraltar have much in common.'

'I don't know. I'm beginning to wonder whether I've met my match.' She looked suddenly appalled. 'I've been out there, Jocelyn, in my nightie, begging that Erl King's Daughter *not* to return to Germany just yet. But I *want* her to go. She *must* go.'

To her surprise he looked rather relieved. 'I think perhaps you ought to let her stay. You can do with some help, and after all Gaylord *did* get her over here, and she seems a nice kid, and–'

'And she treats authors with the adulation due to them,' May said dryly.

'Yes. Well – I should give her a trial, May.'

'If you think so, dear, of course I will,' said May, unusually submissive. 'So perhaps you ought to be getting up, Jocelyn.'

'Getting up? What on earth for?'

'To see to all the formalities. It's sure to be a lengthy business.'

'Formalities?' It was a word Jocelyn hated and dreaded.

She laughed. 'Darling, don't look so shocked. I'm sure the Department of Employment will tell you just what you have to do. They'll even show you how to fill up the various forms if you're in any doubt.' She watched him closely, and saw him blanch. Dear Jocelyn would abandon almost any project that involved filling up forms.

She remembered something else. 'Oh, and I believe you have to arrange for her to have English lessons in the afternoons.'

'My dear May, where on earth could she have English lessons in Shepherd's Warning?'

'Oh, don't ask me. *I'll* teach her to make Yorkshire pudding and toad-in-the-hole. You must – ah, why don't you go and see old Miss Ferris?' she asked cruelly, remembering a teacher from Jocelyn's prep school, now living in retirement in Shepherd's Warning, to avoid whose fearsome demeanour the adult Jocelyn would still dive down a side-street.

Jocelyn said, 'I'd no idea we had to do all this. I'd imagine she could just stay and help.'

She gave him a look, which, while loving, made him feel slightly retarded. And he'd been going to have such a quiet, useful day! Another chapter of his novel. A bit of research. But now? Civil servants, form-filling, the dreaded Miss Ferris glaring down at him (Miss Ferris had the ability to glare down at any of her ex-pupils even if they were, like Jocelyn, nearly six feet). 'It all sounds a bit difficult,' he said.

'You mean you'd rather she didn't stay?'

'I think so,' he said miserably.

May said, 'Very well, dear. If that's how you feel perhaps you'll have a word with her. It might be as well to say we really can't do with her after Friday. Now, what time is it? Still only seven-thirty-five? I might as well go and have my bath.'

Had someone told Amanda Pope's dictum about the proper study of mankind being man, she would have said that the old Pope, whoever he might be, knew what he was talking about. For Amanda's proper study were her elders. She watched them like a chaperon watching a stately dance – the setting to partners, the withdrawing, the bowing, the regrouping, the exchange of glances and smiles and frowns. She missed nothing.

She also knew that whenever *anything* interesting was happening or about to happen, the grown ups immediately closed ranks in order to keep Amanda in complete ignorance.

Amanda thought this was unnecessary, unfriendly, and absolutely foul. But she knew it was no use arguing. When had a grown up ever listened to a ten-year-old? So she took her own steps. Undeclared war. She stifled any conscience she might have had about listening at keyholes, lurking in corners, eavesdropping. A girl just *had* to know what was going on, by fair means or foul.

So, since her bedroom adjoined her parents', and since all the windows were open this lovely morning, she managed, by leaning well out, to hear every word of this conversation. And afterwards she sat on her bedroom window-ledge hugging herself. As self-appointed leader of the *Christine Must Go* party, she'd got another recruit – Daddy. Gaylord was on his own, now, a minority of one.

Nevertheless, Amanda was a realist. Daddy she regarded as a nice chap, but weak and vacillating. Mummy was the one who mattered. Amanda would leave nothing to chance. She put on her friendliest smile, and went and found Christine.

Returning from her bath May heard an unexpected sound: the brisk, efficient clatter of a typewriter.

She went into the little room where she did her typing.

Christine's fingers were moving over the keys. Amanda was reading out to her the letter Jocelyn had yesterday asked May to type. Amanda smiled lovingly at her mother.

'Hello, Mummy. I remembered this letter Daddy asked you to type yesterday. I knew you must have forgotten about it, so I asked Christine to do it. And she's a super typist, Mummy, even in English.'

May, in an old bath robe, and with a waterproof cap on her head, and knowing she *had* forgotten all about the letter, and realizing that Christine sounded a far more assured typist than she, was furious: with the German girl, with Amanda, and with herself, in ascending order.

Christine pulled the letter out of the machine, rose and presented it to May. 'See. The spacing is good, yes? All is in order?'

It was perfect. 'Very nice,' said May. 'And I see you took a copy.'

'Of course. So. I put the letter on Herr Pentecost's desk for signature. And later, when he has approved, I file the copy.'

Amanda said, 'I bet Daddy won't half be impressed. Don't *you* think Daddy will be impressed, Mummy?'

'Very,' said May. She went back to the bedroom. She said, 'I'm sorry, Jocelyn. I forgot to type that letter to the publishers.'

'That's all right, old girl. I knew you'd got other things on your mind.'

She said, 'Miss Haldt's typed it. This morning.'

'Oh, good for her. Is it fit to send?'

'Fit? It's perfect.' She was silent. Then she

said, slowly, 'You know, darling, I think that young woman's beginning to sap my morale.'

May came downstairs at 8.29, to be greeted in the hall by a delighted Christine. 'See Mrs Pentecost, all is prepared.' She led her into the dining room.

May looked at the table: cups, saucers, plates, knives, butter, marmalade, a gurgling coffee percolator – and about fifty slices of toast. Christine said, 'Alas, the baker does not bring the croissants and rolls. So I make toast. Otherwise, all is in order.'

May put an arm about the girl's shoulders. 'I'm afraid it isn't, Christine.'

The girl looked at her piteously. 'Again I do wrong?'

'No, my dear. Not wrong. It's just that if my father-in-law only had toast for breakfast, he'd be showing signs of malnutrition by lunch time.'

'But the baker does not bring the croissants, Frau Pentecost.'

'I don't mean croissants. I mean porridge, eggs, bacon and sausage. And *then* toast and marmalade.'

Christine was silent. Then she turned and marched resolutely towards the kitchen. 'Eggs I know, bacon I know, sausage I know. Porridge I do not know. Please, Mrs Pentecost, *what* is porridge?'

'Well, you take some oatmeal, pour boiling

water on it, and cook for five minutes.'

'It is for horses,' Christine said disgustedly.

'No. That's oats. Look, this is oatmeal.'

Christine looked. 'And you boil?'

'Yes.'

'Then you eat?'

'Yes.'

Christine searched May's face for signs of an English joke, saw none. 'My God,' she said.

'It's really very nice,' May said weakly.

Grandpa erupted into the kitchen. He had entered the dining room as usual – and had seen, with incredulous eyes, a breakfast table laid without forks or porridge spoons, a table in fact that bore all the marks of that lazy, effete and typically foreign hotchpotch, the Continental Breakfast. Well, by George, he wasn't having any of that nonsense. Miss Haldt was a nice girl, and it was pleasant having her about the place, but if she thought she could revolutionize the eating habits of a lifetime, then the sooner she got back to Germany the better. 'May! Where's my porridge?'

'Don't just panic, Father-in-law,' May said coolly. 'Miss Haldt's just preparing it.'

'Oh. Morning, Miss Haldt,' he said, seeing her for the first time. She gave him a bright smile and – what really made his day – a quick curtsey. And she had changed into the pretty bodice and skirt and apron of her

85

native Bavaria. It really *was* pleasant to have her about the place. He said, with one of his rare smiles: 'Thought for a minute you were going to feed me on toast, Miss Haldt.'

'I was,' said the honest Christine. 'But Mrs Pentecost tells me that first you eat the oats.' She peered with distaste into the saucepan she was stirring. 'It is sufficiently boiled, Mrs Pentecost?'

'Yes. That will do, dear. Now go and sit down, Father-in-law. Christine will bring you your porridge.'

He went into the dining room, sat down at the head of the table. Christine came in with a tray containing a dish of porridge and a spoon. She set the dish before him, gave the spoon an elegant wipe on her apron, set it beside the dish, took his napkin, flicked it open and laid it across his knee. *'Guten Appetit!'* she said with another quick curtsey.

John Pentecost was enchanted. Charm, courtesy, deference to age, how seldom did you find these qualities nowadays! Or even a neat and attractive appearance! Yet here they all were, in the person of this delightful young Frawleen. He did hope May wasn't going to be difficult about letting her stay for a bit. Do them all good. Broaden their outlook. There were times, he had to admit, when he suspected Jocelyn of being a bit insular.

CHAPTER 7

Christine really did look pretty in her Bavarian clothes. After breakfast Gaylord decided it was his duty to entertain her.

He came up against two formidable obstacles: a German conscience, and his mother.

'Would you like me to show you round the farm, Christine?' he asked, folding his napkin.

'Very nice of you, Gaylord,' his mother said firmly. 'But I think Miss Haldt wants to learn our household ways. Don't you, Christine?'

'Yes, indeed, Mrs Pentecost. I wish also to be helpful in the extreme.'

'But you said she couldn't stay as an au pair.'

Christine was already piling things urgently on to a tray. She paused only to say, 'At what time does Roger Miles call?'

'Oh, he didn't say. Old Roger never believes in tying himself down.'

Christine looked disappointed – perhaps at such deplorable casualness in her English friends. She picked up the heavily loaded tray, and marched into the kitchen.

Gaylord wandered moodily into the living

room, where Grandpa was represented by an open copy of *The Times*, eight fingers, and a pair of carpet slippers. Then an extraordinary thing happened. Apparently quite unconnected with anything that might be going on in Gaylord's mind, Gaylord's voice said, 'Do you believe in mixed marriages, Grandpa?'

'No,' said Grandpa, burrowing down even deeper behind *The Times*.

Gaylord went and gazed out of the window. 'Lot's of people do.' He searched for a concrete example. 'Othello did.'

'Not for long he didn't,' said Grandpa.

Gaylord fidgeted with the French window key. 'I don't see what's wrong with mixed marriages,' he said.

The old man lowered his paper, glared irritably. 'Stands to sense. Marriage is a bally lottery any way. But if you go for some boot-polished female with a ring through her nose, you're lengthening the odds a thousandfold.'

'I didn't mean some boot-polished female. I meant – French say, or German.'

'Same thing. Nothing like the English rose, my boy: damn fine complexion; honest, God-fearing, *and* you get sensible cooking, none of your foreign messes.' Something struck him. He looked at his own astuteness. 'Good Lord, you've got Christine in your sights.'

'No I haven't.'

''Course you have.'

'Of course I haven't. It was purely a hypothetical question.'

'Hypothetical my foot! Right. Now she's a very charming and attractive young woman, and I must admit if I were your age– But they don't keep their looks, you know.'

'That's Latins.'

The old man shook his head. 'All foreigners. Besides, you mark my words. Marry that girl, and what would happen? He paused dramatically. *'Within six months you'd be on Continental Breakfasts seven days a week.'*

It occurred to Gaylord, delightfully, that being married to Christine might be worth Continental Breakfast seven days a week. But since his question had been purely hypothetical he couldn't very well say so. Besides, the old man hadn't finished. *'And* she'd be calling the kids Siegfried and Gottfried and Wolfgang. Imagine! Gottfried Pentecost!' He brooded. He knew there was a clinching argument somewhere if only he could find it.

He found it. 'They are a nation,' he said in measured terms, 'who play neither cricket or Rugby football. Could you honestly contemplate,' he concluded, 'being married to a woman who doesn't know a touchdown from a googly?' There could be no more argument. He retired behind his paper.

89

Gaylord usually spent his mornings in exhausting activity. Today he hung about the kitchen, drying a cup here, putting away a fork there, until his exasperated mother said, 'Oh, go and get some fresh air for heaven's sake.'

'In Germany,' Christine said to May, 'The young men are very active, climbing upon the mountains, singing as they stride through the forest, out in the sunlight the livelong day.'

'I was only trying to be useful,' said Gaylord, hurt.

'Off you go, dear,' said May.

He wandered up to his room. There was really nothing he wanted to do, until Roger arrived. Rowing or cycling on your own were very lonely occupations. And he didn't really feel very energetic. If the truth were known, he thought, I'm sickening for something. He clasped his forehead; hot. It was a bit heartless, he thought, being turned out of the house when you were ill, perhaps dying. He only hoped his mother would be duly remorseful when– And that conjured up a sad but rather delightful picture of the black-robed priest administering the last rites (a picture that would have horrified the Shepherd's Warning Vicar, a cleric of decidedly Evangelical convictions), while his mother tried pathetically to make up for her heartlessness, and Christine Haldt, in a blue négligé, lovingly wiped the sweat from his pale brow.

Perhaps the best thing would be to sit quietly in the orchard and read a book. He was in the middle of a very exciting Hornblower. But – something that had never occurred to him before – there were no women in it. And a book without women in it, he thought severely, dealt with only half of life. So instead he took Shakespeare's Romeo and Juliet to see what the Bard, who was generally considered fairly knowledgeable on the subject, had to say about love.

A low seat was set against the trunk of a gnarled old pear tree. He sat down and began to read.

After a time he heard footsteps. 'What do you read?' said a voice.

'Christine!' He sprang to his feet, beaming. 'Sit down. Oh, just a moment.' He carefully dusted the old seat with his handkerchief.

She smiled. 'Thank you.' She sat down. 'From which direction comes Mr Miles?'

'Along the river road. There. If he comes. But of course, he's awfully busy. His father has the Swan Hotel in Ingerby. And Roger helps a lot during the holidays.' Gaylord spent a few moments marvelling at the thought of someone of Roger's eminence helping in a hotel. He said, 'He was Captain of the School, you know. And he's going up to Oxford.'

'So you said.'

'*And* he was Captain of Cricket and Rugger.' He remembered his grandfather's words. 'You – er – know about cricket and rugger?'

'Yes. Before I come to England I study all English games. The clock golf, the Rugby (League and Union), the table tennis, the netball, the cricket.' She checked them off on her fingers in what Gaylord thought a most delightful manner. 'The Rugby League is a fast and clean game. The Rugby Union is pointless and incomprehensible. The cricket game lasts three days and is susceptible to the weather, and since there are never three consecutive fine days in England no game is ever finished. The clock golf–'

'Actually you are not quite right about Rugby,' said Gaylord, whose lovely companion had unwittingly stung him to the quick. 'Rugby Union is a far better game. It started at Rugby school. League is a very poor imitation.'

'You have played both?'

'Great Scott, no.'

'Ah. But you have watched both?'

'Actually, no.'

'Then how do you know? *Englishman*,' she added with sudden scorn.

He could not have been more startled had she struck him. He was silent. 'So,' she cried triumphantly, 'It is as my book says. In England there is much snobbery about

Rugby football. I do not like snobbery.'

He was silent for a long time. Then he said, 'You know, you're right. It hadn't occurred to me.'

She looked at him thoughtfully. 'I imagine very little occurs to you English. You live in your little island, where Rugby Union and porridge for breakfast and stiff upper lips are good; and Rugby League, and coffee and croissants, and bosoms before breakfast are bad.'

He was beginning to see the middle-class English in a new, and not very pleasant, light. But he didn't really want to think about such things. Christine was very close, and very pretty. And though he couldn't approve of her criticizing the English – it was one thing for the English to criticize themselves, but even the nicest foreigners ought to know their place – he nevertheless felt very tender towards her. He edged a little closer. She looked at him, and smiled, but did not move away. Terribly brave, he took her hand. She made as though to withdraw it; then let it lie in his. He wondered, panic stricken, what he was suppose to do next.

To his delight she put her head rather close to his and murmured. 'But I will not chastise. *When* comes the Captain Miles?'

'I thought he'd have been here by now if he was coming,' said Gaylord.

'Oh! You really think he may not come?'

she said wistfully.

Gaylord, to whom loyalty was a basic principle, was horrified to find himself rather hoping Miles *wouldn't* come. It was incredible. He just didn't know what had happened to him.

Meanwhile her hand was smooth and warm, and exquisitely alive. This contact was very heaven. He would have sat so, the livelong day, asking nothing more, the sun warm and caressing on his bare arms, young love warm and generous in his heart. Occasionally Christine would glance at him and smile, half amused, half tender, then look down at the orchard grass. If this could last forever! thought Gaylord.

But it couldn't. He heard the swish of someone walking through the long grass; and had just time to move a foot away from Christine, and drop her hand as though it were a hot potato, before Amanda appeared. (Kid sisters must not be allowed to catch elder brothers in compromising situations. When it comes to retentiveness of memory, thought Gaylord, kid sisters beat elephants hollow.)

'Hello, Gaylord,' Amanda said sweetly. 'Got tired of holding hands?'

Gaylord went very red while he considered various tactics: denial, innocent incomprehension, contempt. He chose the last. 'Loathsome child,' he murmured loftily.

'Well, you were, weren't you. I went past five minutes ago, doing my Big Chief Sitting Bull.'

'What is your Big Chief Sitting Bull?' inquired Christine with interest.

'You crawl with your belly in the long grass,' said Amanda coldly. She didn't see why she should spend her mornings improving the English of someone who was clearly bent on stealing Gaylord from her.

'For what purpose?'

'To spy on her betters,' Gaylord said, glaring at Amanda.

'Spying I do not like,' said Christine. 'But why is it so called? It is an English idiom?'

Amanda gave a weary and long-suffering sigh. Gaylord tried to hide her rudeness with his own courtesy. 'It's what Red Indians do, Christine.'

'So. But *why* is it so called?'

'Well, Big Chief—' It was very difficult. *'Der gross Oberhaupt sitzend Bulle* – He was a famous Indian Chief,' he finished lamely.

'So. But in England there are no Red Indians, surely?'

'I wish there were,' muttered Amanda. 'There might be a chance of some people getting scalped.'

Christine turned to Gaylord. 'What does the child say?'

It occurred to Gaylord that any relationship that might have formed between the

95

German girl and his sister didn't look like coming into the beautiful friendship class. 'Run along, Amanda,' he said quietly.

'Why?' said Amanda.

'I'm sure Mum needs some help.'

'She doesn't. Christine's done it all.' She gave the German girl a smile of pure sweetness. 'Haven't you, Christine?'

Porridge, the inexplicable connection between Red Indians and an English orchard, the unfulfilled promise of Roger Miles, a flat landscape, the English shock and horror at the thought of anyone doing *anything* before eight o'clock in the morning, a casual and unenthusiastic reception from everyone except this boy Gaylord, who was a bit too enthusiastic – Christine said, 'I think I go home. England is too difficult.'

Amanda's features did not change. But her nostrils flared for a moment like a tennis player who has broken her opponent's first service.

Gaylord, on the other hand, was appalled and bewildered. 'Difficult? There is nothing difficult about us. We're terribly easy to get on with.'

'I do not mean to get on with. I mean to understand.' She saw Amanda's narrow, amused eyes watching her and Gaylord, revelling in this scene. The sight seemed to make her very angry. 'You are upside-down people, in the looking glass, like your Alice,

96

a children's book which they tell me at the Gymnasium you rank with the Bible and Shakespeare. And always you make English jokes. Always, always, always.'

In anger, her eyes were not only beautiful. They were magnificent. Gaylord said quietly, 'Not always, Christine. We're not making them now. And – we're sorry if we've laughed at things you don't understand. Aren't we, Amanda?'

'I suppose so,' said Amanda, a little hoity-toity. She had got to foil Gaylord's attempts to change the girl's mind for her. Gaylord was *her* property, her adored, cheerful big brother who romped and played with her like a sheep dog with a small terrier.

But Christine stayed unmollified. 'I go home,' she said. 'To the mountains and the great forests.'

'No,' pleaded Gaylord. He put an arm about her shoulders. She shook him off.

'Look,' he said. 'Let's talk it over.' And was aware that if they did talk it over, it would be under the relentless gaze of Amanda. 'So long, Mandy,' he said, sounding more hopeful than he felt.

'Oh, there's no hurry,' said Amanda. She sat herself on to the seat between Gaylord and Christine. 'Now,' she said cosily, 'Let's talk it over.' But to herself she said, 'Check!'

Gaylord said, 'Don't you think you'd feel rather silly going home again after three days, when they were expecting you to be away indefinitely?'

Christine hung her head. She said, 'My mother does not know I am au pairing in England. She has forbidden it.'

Gaylord looked at her in amazement. 'Where *does* she think you are?'

'Youth hostelling in the Harz mountains.' She looked troubled. 'That again is why I wish to return home. I am by nature honest, and am not prepared to continue a deceit when it brings me little pleasure.'

Amanda said, 'You mean – you told your mum you were going youth hostelling, and came au pairing instead?'

'Yes.' said Christine, subdued and ashamed.

'Cor!' said Amanda, looking at her enemy with a new respect, admiration even. 'I bet she won't half be livid when she finds out.'

'That is why I must return, and confess my transgression.'

'Wouldn't like to be in your shoes,' said Amanda. 'Still, the longer you stay the worse it will be, I can see that.'

Gaylord said, 'Suppose my mother wrote to yours, explained things–?'

Christine shook her head.

'Only make things worse,' Amanda said judicially. She turned on Christine a look of sympathy and deep understanding. 'I bet you're homesick, too. All those mountains and forests. I bet this lot doesn't half seem flat.'

'It does, rather.'

Amanda looked at the power station across the valley. 'I bet you can't see *one* of those from where you live.'

'Stop saying, "I bet",' Gaylord said irritably. He'd got a sufficiently uphill struggle without young Amanda chipping in on the other side.

Christine turned on him 'Why should she not say, "I bet"? It is common?'

'No. But one just doesn't.'

Christine gave him a look. Amanda said, 'From the top meadow you can see five power stations all at once.'

'From a point near my home,' Christine said wistfully, 'you can see the Zugspitze and the great peaks of the Bayerische Alpen.'

'Whatever made you come to the English Midlands?' Amanda said.

'That is what I ask myself,' said Christine.

CHAPTER 8

'Your tiny hand is frozen. Let me warm it into life,' growled Charles Bunting tunelessly as he gathered together his brushes and paints. *La vie de bohème*, he thought wryly as he stowed them in the boot of the Rolls. Henri Murger wouldn't approve. But then, there were no Mimis, coughing their hearts up in the Trent Valley. Only other men's wives, in twin sets and pearls. So an artist was entitled to console himself with a vintage Rolls, surely. *Cueillez dès aujourd'hui les roses de la vie.* And a Rolls Royce was a *rose de la vie* some men would sell their souls to the devil for.

'Hey, Liz,' he called. 'Don't forget we're going to the Pentecosts' for lunch.'

'I'm not going,' said Liz, wan.

"Course you're going. What's the matter? Had a tiff–?' He looked at her closely. 'It's nothing to do with Gaylord making a pass at the Erl King's daughter, is it?'

Liz said indignantly, 'He *didn't* make a pass. He only kissed her hand.'

He grinned, teasingly. 'I bet he's never kissed *your* grubby little paw.'

'I resent that remark,' Liz said coldly.

Oh, Lord, he thought. Love, and adolescence! What they can do to even the most amiable characters! He said contritely, 'Sorry, old girl.' He tried to cheer her with an old joke. 'Never could open my mouth without putting my foot in it.'

She was not amused. 'Come on! A little smile,' he wheedled, going down on his haunches, smiling up into her face.

She looked at him coldly. Then slowly,

reluctantly, she gave him a sad smile. 'He's sure to fall in love with her, Father.'

'Of course he's not. Why should he, with a nice English girl like you around?'

'Every reason. She's good looking, and ever so intelligent and charming–'

'So are you, my love.'

'Father, I'm *not*. Anyway,' she said miserably, 'he doesn't see me as feminine at all. I thought, for a minute, yesterday evening, he did. But then *she* turned up.'

He had straightened up now, was staring out of the window at the blues and greens and subtleties of colour that made up his artist's world. 'So you think that to leave her with a clear field today is the best way to win this race?' he said thoughtfully.

She was silent. Then she said, 'It wouldn't make any difference if I did go. He'd never even notice me. It would just be – painful.'

'And you'd rather not risk getting hurt?'

'Yes. I would. When there's no point in it.'

He came back to her. He said, 'Being cowardly and defeatist is no way to win a race, or a battle, or a boyfriend, Liz.'

She flushed violently. But said nothing.

He said, 'That was cruel, and I'm sorry.' He was, too. And he thought angrily: I seem to spend half my life being sorry because I've hurt somebody.

'That's all right,' said Liz, doing her best to rustle up a forgiving smile.

'And you'll go for lunch?'

'No,' she said.

'I see,' he said, without emotion. He went and climbed into the Rolls.

Liz knew the utter misery of youth. Her father despised her, and if she stayed at home he would despise her even more; and, frankly, she'd only be cutting off her nose to spite her face. Yet suppose she went, and her dear Gaylord was too taken up with the German girl even to notice her? It would be an agonizing day. But so it would be if she stayed at home and imagined Gaylord and his German love together.

She heard the engine of the Rolls begin to purr. Matters were being taken out of her hands. The scrunch of tyres on the gravel, a touch of the horn in farewell. Father believed in letting you make up your own mind.

It was a lovely day. And a meal at the Pentecosts was always fun. She had never felt more lonely in her life.

May was putting in a bit of typing when the telephone rang. 'Mrs Pentecost? Liz here. I'm ever so sorry, Mrs Pentecost, but I can't come for lunch today.'

'Oh, Liz, I *am* sorry.' The girl sounded fraught. 'Nothing wrong, is there?'

'No. Just a bit off colour. Daddy's on his way.'

'So you're all alone?'

'Yes. But that's all right.'

'Poor old Liz. I'll telephone you later. See if there's anything I can do.'

'Thanks, Mrs Pentecost.' She put down the receiver. Now what was all that about? thought May (Jocelyn said she had a habit of putting two and two together and making six, instead of taking things at their face value. But it was surprising how often two and two *did* make six).

She went back to her typewriter. Christine Haldt burst in. 'Mrs Pentecost, I go back to Germany,' she announced dramatically.

'Very well, dear,' said May, looking up for a moment and smiling. 'Will you have lunch first, or are you going straight off?'

Christine looked surprised and deflated. Then she gave a rather rueful grin. 'I *am* hungry.'

'Good. About one o'clock then.' She returned to her typing once more.

Christine went up to her room, reflecting that it wasn't surprising so few operas had English settings. Trying to be dramatic with the English was like trying to strike a match on a damp box.

May pushed her glasses a bit higher up her nose, and went on typing. Charles came in.

'Charles!' She rose, smiling, took off her glasses.

'Don't take 'em off,' he said. 'They suit you.'

'Rubbish! What's wrong with Liz? She's just telephoned. A certain wanness, I felt.'

He went and perched on the side of her typing table. 'Adolescence. Love. The Erl King's Daughter.'

'Meaning–?'

'She's in love. With young Gaylord. And she thinks the German girl's going to spirit him away from her. And she hadn't the guts to come and fight for him.'

'That's cruel, Charles. She's just too nice to be a fighter.'

She looked at his dark, hungry features. And saw pain in them. 'It's love that's cruel, May. Not me.'

He was watching her closely. She said hurriedly, 'I must get lunch moving. Go and help yourself to a drink, Charles.'

'Thanks.' He straightened up lazily, went and opened the door for her. 'Do you know your Ronsard? *Ronsard me célébrait du temps que j'étais belle.*'

She looked at him coolly. 'Does that mean you've brought your paints?'

'Yes,' he said. 'And it means more than that.' She wished he'd stop staring at her. She was uneasy. Her woman's instinct had warned her about this portrait business. She'd only agreed because Jocelyn seemed to want it. And now it was too late to say no.

Just as they were finishing lunch Amanda leapt from her chair, muttered, ''Scuse me,' and tore from the room, uttering glad cries.

'Amanda!' May called angrily. 'Come back!'

'Too late! That child's getting out of hand,' said Jocelyn. 'I'll speak to her.'

Christine looked at him with respect. 'It is good to see the Father showing authority.' Jocelyn looked like a spaniel that has just been patted on the head.

'Do that,' said May. 'I will not tolerate bad manners. Especially when we have a foreign guest.' She smiled charmingly at Christine. 'And at your last meal with us, too.'

'It is of no account,' said Christine. 'In Germany, too, it is said, there is coming a breakdown of parental authority.'

'Last meal?' said Grandpa, who had a bad habit, which could be irritating, of latching on to the last remark but one.

'Miss Haldt has decided to return home,' said May. And I can't say I'm sorry, she thought. Breakdown of parental authority, indeed!

'My dear Miss Haldt,' said Grandpa, who had already been looking forward to a succession of breakfasts served by a pretty Bavarian. 'Can we not persuade you–?'

Gaylord went very pink. He said, 'Well, *I* think it's rotten, sending Christine back just because you've changed your mind about having an au pair girl.'

May said, 'My dear boy, circumstances

change in ten years.'

'I don't see how,' said Gaylord crossly.

'Don't speak to your mother like that,' said Jocelyn, hoping to earn for himself a new slice of respect from Christine.

Gaylord scowled. Christine said severely, 'At home, if a boy spoke to his mother so, he would be sent out into the barn to saw logs.'

'I'm *not* a boy.'

'No. You're behaving like a child of seven,' said his mother. But that was all the time she had for Gaylord when he was in this mood. She turned to her other guest. 'Charles, it's too glorious a day to be indoors. Couldn't you paint me out of doors?' (She'd feel safer outside.)

'No.'

'Why not?'

'The light for one thing.'

'Well, Leonardo managed it. Mona Lisa looks as though she's halfway up the mountainside.'

'You simply don't understand how an artist works,' he said crossly. 'That's obvious.'

She changed tack. *'Please, Charles,* I hate being indoors when I could be out.'

'Oh, all right,' he said ungraciously. 'I suppose so.'

'Good. Bless you, Charles. You are sweet.' She rewarded him with a charming smile. 'Now. Just wait while I wash these dishes and tart myself up and I'll be with you.'

He was appalled. 'I don't *want* you with a lot of muck on your face. I want you natural.'

'You'll have muck or nothing. Au naturel, I look ninety.'

'Rubbish!'

'It's perfectly true. Isn't it, Jocelyn.'

'What's that, old girl?'

'Oh, nothing.'

Christine said, 'I will wash up, Mrs Pentecost, while you paint your face.'

'I'll help you, Miss Haldt,' said Charles.

'And *I* will,' said Gaylord, reflecting sadly that he couldn't see Shelley or Byron spending their last hours with the beloved washing dinner pots. But for him it was that or nothing.

Christine smiled delightfully on them both. 'I will show you how we wash up in Germany,' she promised. 'Here I imagine you are perhaps not so well organized.'

'That will be a veritable treat,' said Charles. But at that moment the door was flung open and Amanda entered, swinging delightedly on the arm of Roger Miles.

Amanda, from her seat at table, had seen a tiny, distant figure on the river road, and had known it for her adored Roger. Hence her unorthodox departure. She ran, hair flying, along the road, arms outstretched. Faster, faster, she went.

Roger stopped his bicycle. He couldn't

have done much else without running Amanda down. She flung herself into his arms. 'Roger! Miss Haldt's here, and Gaylord's getting all soppy about her only I don't think I want him to much. Can I ride on the cross bar?'

He hoisted her up, and pedalled on. She gazed into his face. 'I do love you, Roger. You *will* wait for me, won't you.'

'Naturally.'

'I know you seem a lot older now, but when I'm eighty you'll only be eighty-seven.' She pondered. 'I don't think I could ever catch you up, though, could I?'

'I think you might if we travelled faster than light. Something to do with Einstein. I'm not sure though.'

'Pedal as fast as you can, and see what happens.'

He pedalled furiously. It was exciting, clinging to his strong left arm, with the road whizzing past beneath her. But she couldn't say she felt any older. 'Do *you* feel any younger, Roger?'

'I think I do a bit,' he panted.

'How much younger?'

'About five minutes.'

'Miss Haldt says she's going back to Germany. I don't think she likes us lot much.'

'Why *ever* not.' It had never occurred to him that anyone could *not* like the middle class English. A class, and a breed, whose natural charm was never stinted when dealing with someone of another class or another nation, who always, in the finest English tradition, went out of their way to put foreigners, tradesmen and workpeople at their ease. Not like *us?* 'Why ever not?' he said again.

'Dunno. Are you still getting younger?'

'Every minute.' But his mind was on this extraordinary business of Miss Haldt. The Pentecosts must have been pretty ham-fisted in some way. It was a good job, he thought, that he'd come over this afternoon to put things right. It wouldn't take *him* long. We couldn't have a German chick going back and poisoning the minds of other German chicks against the English. Roger thought it important that all the world's chicks – German, French, American, Spanish – should love the English. He fully expected chicks to play an important part in his life for the next ten years or so.

'Hello, Miles,' said Gaylord, as one might say, 'Hail Caesar.'

'Hello, Roger,' said May. 'Join us for coffee?'

'Thank you, Mrs Pentecost.' She felt herself blossoming under his smile. Ridiculous woman, she thought. Someone less than half my age, my son's friend, and if I don't

109

watch myself I shall get all coy.

Amanda said, with a rather pathetic pride, 'He *is* dishy, isn't he?'

He was, too. His white tennis shirt and shorts set off his sleek hair and his suntan splendidly.

'Very dishy,' said May, smiling up at him. She said, 'Christine, I think you have met Roger.'

'Hi,' said Roger, waving his tennis racket at her. Christine inclined her head with the dignity of a Frau General. 'Hi,' she said, rather spoiling the effect, and she coloured deeply.

'Thought we might have a foursome,' said Roger. 'You said you played, Miss Haldt?'

'Yes. My tennis is not brilliant, but it is sound.'

'But you're going back to Germany.' Amanda almost squeaked in her fury. Hell, she thought. One sight of my darling Roger and she's prepared to stay the winter. She is not content with pinching Gaylord. She's after Roger as well now. Christine smiled sweetly at Roger. 'Oh, I do not think a game of tennis will make so much difference.'

''Course it won't,' said Roger.

'Of course it won't,' said Gaylord, delighted by this reprieve. 'Who's the fourth?'

'Oh, I imagined young Liz Bunting was here.' Roger looked put out. 'Give her a ring, Gaylord. Won't take her long to get over here on her bike.'

May said, 'It's just possible she won't obey the command. She wasn't feeling well, poor kid.'

'I'll play,' said Amanda.

'You can be ball boy,' Roger said kindly.

'If you don't let me play I shall marry someone else when I grow up.' Then, since Roger looked quite unshaken by this fearful threat, she stuck her lower lip out, nodded towards Christine, and said, 'I bet I can play as well as her, anyway. I bet *we* were playing tennis when *they* were still hacking each other to bits with iron swords.'

The moment she had spoken she looked fearful but unrepentant.

'Amanda!' cried May in the voice she used only when Amanda had gone Too Far. 'Apologize at once.'

Gaylord said, 'I'm sorry, Christine. Just ignore the revolting child.'

But it was clear that Christine's recent commendation had gone to Jocelyn's head. He said, quietly but fiercely, 'Go to your room, Amanda. And don't dare to cross that threshold again until I give you permission.'

For a moment Amanda stood staring at her father. She quivered with rage. She really looked as though her small frame might explode with anger. Then she flounced out of the room. Going upstairs she managed to sound like a sixteen-stone man in hobnail boots.

Grandpa looked severely at his son. 'You've upset her, Jocelyn.'

'She needed upsetting,' May said grimly.

But Christine's eyes were shining. 'Bravo, Mr Pentecost!' She explained: 'I think to myself, the Father is a great author, and is therefore to be revered. But what a pity that, like all English fathers, he has no authority over his wife and children. So I think; and so I revere him less. But now I see that, with this recalcitrant child, you have much authority. And so I revere you more, Herr Pentecost.'

Well, bully for Herr Pentecost, thought May. She said to Christine, 'You go and get ready for tennis. Mr Bunting and I will wash up. Er – I take it you don't *have* to go today after all?'

'Not if you will let me stay until tomorrow,' Christine said, smiling charmingly at May and then at Roger as he held the door for her.

Roger watched her departing back. Then he said, 'Look, old chap. Don't leave it too long to telephone Liz. I am on rather a tight schedule.'

May thought: should I go and have a word with Amanda? No, she thought. Her father was quite right. It'll do her good to let her stew a bit.

Which was perhaps as well, since Amanda was in Christine's room, searching furiously for the girl's home address.

She soon found it, in the lid of a suitcase. She copied it down carefully. Then she went up to her room, took a card decorated with daffodils, and wrote as follows:

The Cypresses Farm,
Shepherd's Warning,
Derbyshire.

Dear Mrs Haldt,
    Your daughter is not in the Hearts Mountains you have been deceived! She is hear!!!
Yours Affec,
A Friend (Amanda Pentecost,)
Miss

She put it in an envelope, addressed it, sealed it, and told herself she must post it before her conscience started asking her whether she wasn't being a bit sneaky. (But of course it wasn't sneaky. All was fair in love and war. Christine was the sneaky one, telling her mother she was off to the Hearts Mountains and then coming here.)
    But how was she going to post it, when Daddy had confined her to barracks? Well, there were more ways of killing a dog than hanging. Still quivering with rage, she looked urgently round her room. Her eyes fell on the bed sheets.

It always distressed Liz to find how little her broken heart affected her appetite. She hard-boiled a couple of eggs, cut three thick slices of bread and butter, placed the eggs in a pretty nest of tomatoes and lettuce and cucumber and radishes, found the remains of an apple pie, opened a bottle of Coke, and carried the whole lot out into the sunshine. She sat down in a little arbour where the sun was a benison and the leaves were a shelter and the silence and solitude were a balm to life's wounds. And here she tucked in, while she wondered what Gaylord and Christine were doing; and she imagined, with an intensity of pain, their kisses, honeysweet in the summer's warmth.

Now mingling with the murmur of bees and the soft sighing of the breeze, came another sound: too faint at first to worm its way into her consciousness. But then, suddenly, it was burrowing through labyrinthine ways into her brain. And her brain was giving sudden orders to glands and nerves and muscles, and she was running toward the house, her whole being mobilized like a warship at action stations. And the telephone bell continued, wearily patient, to summon her.

It stopped ringing just as she reached the back door. She flung herself inside, grabbed the receiver, put it against her ear. 'Hello!' she called. 'Hello!' Only the dialling tone.

She put back the receiver. She mooned

114

back into the sunlight. She wasn't crying, but there were tears at the back of her eyes. Of course, it might not have been Gaylord. But if it *had* been, inviting her over! Suppose he wasn't in love with the German girl after all! And here she was, alone, through her own folly. An afternoon of loneliness stretched before her like eternity.

The 'phone rang again. She tore inside, grabbed the receiver. Her heart was pounding, he would hear it at the other end of the line.

'Hello,' said Gaylord. 'Thought you were out. I rang a few minutes ago.' He sounded reproachful.

'No. I was in the garden. I ran – but I was too late.'

'Oh, that's all right. Look, what about coming over for tennis?'

'Gaylord, I'd love to. Straight away?'

'Yes. Pedal furiously.'

She ran into the garden, snatched up the tray, crammed the remaining boiled egg and a slice of cucumber into her mouth, swigged down the glass of Coke, ran into the house, dumped the dishes on the draining board, changed into tennis clothes, pulled her hair into a pony tail, and was off on her bicycle, singing happily, all in five minutes flat.

She didn't know what had happened to the Erl King's daughter, but clearly she and Gaylord weren't spending the afternoon together. Perhaps he didn't love her after all! Perhaps, the other evening, when he had looked at Liz with sudden interest, something *had* clicked into place and he had suddenly said to himself, 'Liz Bunting! Liz Bunting is the girl for me.' And ten minutes ago she'd been sitting alone, with a glass of Coke, confronting eternity!

The river danced and gurgled. The larks climbed invisible spiral staircases to the sky, singing their heads off. And Liz sang with them as her knees went up and down, up and down, driving her on ecstatically through the soft air.

She came in sight of the farm. Her eyes could focus on nothing else. Soon, now, she might see him if he were out of doors.

She saw him! On the tennis court, with two other people! Her heart sank. It sank even further when she recognized them: Roger Miles, whom she thought conceited. And the German creature. She wobbled violently, and was turning to go home again when Roger Miles spotted her, cupped his hands about his mouth and called, 'Come on, we're waiting for you.'

Play tennis with Roger Miles, who was almost *county* standard? And with Christine, who was sure to be good. Christine, Liz thought with an unusual lack of charity, was one of those odious creatures who do everything well.

CHAPTER 9

This is how the family disposed itself for the long, drowsy summer afternoon.

John Pentecost stumped into the orchard, lowered himself into a deck chair, and enjoyed that delight which, the wise believe, a kindly God created specifically to recompense old men for being old. He snoozed in the sunshine.

Jocelyn, being less old and less wise, sat in his study, and added to the great mountain of unnecessary words that towers high and ever higher above the human race, working as always, this lovely afternoon, with the mindless dedication of the termite, the coral polyp, or the honey bee.

Amanda sat by her window, knotting together her bed sheets with quiet but furious determination. 'Don't dare cross the threshold,' he had said. Right! She wouldn't. But she'd post her letter!

On the tennis court Christine said, 'Roger and I play together, yes?'

'Yes,' said Roger.

'I'm not very good,' said Liz nervously.

Roger served to Liz. He coiled himself

tight, like a spring. He uncoiled. Something shot past Liz at roughly the speed of light. 'Fifteen love,' said Christine.

Roger served to Gaylord. Quite by chance Gaylord's racket happened to be in the way of the ball. The ball knocked it out of Gaylord's hand. At the end of that game Liz, gathering the balls to serve, said, 'I'm not really very good.'

'Never mind,' said Christine kindly. 'It's only a game.'

When Roger and Christine were winning fifty love, fifty love, fifty-fifteen, fifty love, Christine said, 'Who has taught you to play, Liz?'

'Nobody,' said Liz, forlorn.

Christine turned to Roger. 'So. You play with Gaylord. I partner Liz.' She came across to Liz. 'Now, Liebchen, grip the racket so. And hold the right arm, thus. It is not a pat-a-cake we play.' She looked at the racket. 'Alas! It is more like a shrimping net.'

'It was my mother's,' said Liz. She wanted to add, 'And I don't *want* to learn to play. I just wanted to have a foolish, idle afternoon with Gaylord.' But the German girl was being so kind, so helpful, that she couldn't bring herself to say a word.

May, bending over a sinkful of dishes, was curiously aware of being alone with Charles Bunting. Why on earth had she dismissed

118

the German girl so easily? Surely she hadn't, subconsciously, *wanted* this? No. That was absurd.

Out of the corner of her eye she saw that even as he dried a handful of plates he was watching her intently. And now he said suddenly, breaking a long silence: 'A beautiful woman like you shouldn't have to wash dishes.'

'I'm not beautiful,' she said.

'Of course you're beautiful. Oh, for heaven's sake admit it and be thankful for it. It's God's greatest gift to a woman.'

She did not look at him. Staring into the sink she said, 'More than intelligence?'

'Good Lord, yes. No one wants a woman to be intelligent. *And* you know it. That's why you pretend to be so bat-witted on occasion.'

Now she did look at him, her grey eyes large with astonishment. 'But Charles. I don't pretend.'

They stared at each other. Then he said, 'Clever girl! But you don't fool me.' He picked up another pile of plates. 'Have you ever thought what it *means* to be beautiful? That it is something you share with a field of daffodils, and a white horse running in the wind, and a cherry in bloom? That *you* are a part – of all that?'

She said, 'Be careful with this jug. It's got a slight crack.' She was silent for a long time. She said, 'I don't think I want you to paint my portrait, Charles.'

'Why not?' He was angry already.

'I think I'm afraid. I don't want you looking into my soul.'

'My God, woman, this is the most important picture I've ever done. You're not backing out now. I'll see you on the lawn in ten minutes. Here, what do I do with this thing?' He threw the tea towel at her. And was gone.

Very thoughtfully, May went up to her room, and started on her face. I'm being bullied, she thought. And I'm letting him get away with it. Why, why, why? She didn't know. But when, in just ten minutes, she came down to the lawn, there was a wicker chair for her, and a magazine, and he was already angrily slapping paint on to the canvas. 'Sit down,' he said, not looking at her. 'Read that magazine. Got your specs?'

'I don't need glasses,' she said, with a rather shocked laugh.

'Thought you'd taken to 'em. Recently.'

'Yes. Well, I've got a pair for reading. But I don't need them.'

'Well, I do. I want to paint you in them.'

'No.'

He was silent. Then suddenly he began painting again, intent, staring at the canvas, then staring at her, into her, through her, for long minutes. 'Now I know how a beetle feels under a microscope,' she said.

'You'd have looked better in your specs,' he said. 'And just as beautiful.'

Suddenly he strode over to her. She looked up at him, alarmed. There was no doubt she was on edge this afternoon. He seized her right shoulder, pulled it round. 'Now. Your hand in your lap, so. And look over there – at the house.' He stared at her face. 'And for God's sake look serene. What did you think I was going to do? Ravish you?'

'Sorry,' she said meekly. 'You made me jump.' He had, too. Her heart was pounding.

He went back to his easel. He stood, half stooping, and stared at her critically. Then he began to paint again.

Jocelyn came hurrying across the lawn. 'May, Madame Teresa on the telephone. She wants to know whether you can change your hair appointment.'

'Oh, Lord. When to?'

'She didn't say,' said Jocelyn. 'I think you'd better come and have a word with her.'

May looked anxiously at Charles Bunting and half rose. Charles shouted, 'Sit down. Dammit, woman, you wouldn't get up in the middle of having your teeth filled. So why–?'

May said, 'I'm coming, Jocelyn.' She began to follow him. 'Charles, if you don't stop addressing me as "woman", I shall refuse to sit. Now just read "*She*" till I come back. There should be much to interest you.'

When she came back she sat down demurely and said, 'Sorry, Charles.'

He grunted, and went back to his painting. Ten minutes later they heard cries of rage and pain from the orchard.

'Excuse me, Charles,' May said firmly, and hurried off. She found John Pentecost threshing about in agony. 'What is it, Father-in-law?'

His reply, interspersed with pauses when his agony proved too much for him, was to the effect that he had been damn well stung on the wrist.

'Bee or wasp? asked May, trying desperately to remember whether it was acid for bees and alkali for wasps, or vice versa.

'How the devil do I know?'

'I thought you might have seen your assailant. Were you asleep?'

'Of course I wasn't asleep.' John Pentecost never *admitted* to sleeping in the daytime, being very outspoken about some of his contemporaries who indulged in this habit. Letting themselves get old before their time was the way he described it.

May looked at his wrist, tut-tutted, led him carefully into the house, smothered his wrist with TCP, gave him a glass of brandy, took his temperature, and asked him whether he would like to go to bed, and whether she should fetch the doctor. This well-tried ploy of May's, which she referred to privately as

Operation Overkill, was never known to fail. The old gentleman reminded her forcibly that he was neither five nor ninety-five, and that anyone who kept himself as fit as he did could take a wasp sting in his stride, and to prove it he walked sturdily back into the orchard under his own steam.

'Quite finished?' Charles demanded nastily.

'Yes, thank you, Charles,' said May sweetly, rearranging herself.

He tried again. Oh, it was lovely sitting there, the sun burning into her cheek. The only sounds came from the toiling bees, the ecstatic larks. So she sat, blessed in the knowledge that it was her *duty*, for a whole afternoon, to do *nothing*; to do nothing, to think of nothing, simply to be. Simply to *be*, she thought with sudden pride, herself, May Pentecost, whom some thought beautiful. Her head fell forward on to her breast.

A cold voice said, 'I'm not doing the Sleeping Beauty. I'm doing Mrs Jocelyn Pentecost.

She jerked up. 'Sorry, Charles.' She fixed her gaze on the house.

'I should damn well think so," he said.

She was terrified she would actually drop off. But now she became aware of something that ensured her wakefulness. A white snake was slithering out of one of the bedroom windows and slowly crawling down the side of the house.

May stared in wonder. It was Amanda's room. So *anything* could be happening.

It wasn't a snake. It was bed sheets knotted together. The house couldn't be on fire? Or could it? She was on her feet. Amanda's face appeared at the window. 'Mandy,' May yelled. 'What are you doing?'

'Escaping,' said Amanda in a tone of disgust.

'Escaping from what?' cried May.

There was no reply. Amanda's head had disappeared. But now her left leg was flung over the window sill. It was too much. May set off for the house.

It was too much for somebody else. Strong exasperated hands seized her shoulders, spun her round, marched her back to her chair. 'How *dare* you?' she cried. 'Charles, how–?'

He silenced her by the quite unpremeditated action of snatching her to him, covering her mouth with his, and kissing her with sudden hunger.

May brought her hand up through a ninety-degree arc and slapped his cheek. The sound of the slap rang through the quiet afternoon like a pistol shot. It even woke John Pentecost.

Amanda, astride the window ledge and reaching for the sheet rope, nearly fell out of the window. She didn't quite understand

124

what defending one's honour meant, but clearly Mummy was doing it. This was even better than escaping. She climbed back into her bedroom and legged it for her father's study. 'Daddy?'

Jocelyn, already put back a couple of paragraphs by Madame Teresa, did not look overjoyed to see his daughter. Besides, he always felt very relieved that his children usually obeyed him, since he knew he wouldn't have a clue if they defied him. And here *was* defiance! He said, with far more confidence than he felt: 'I told you–'

'I know. But Mummy's defending her honour. I thought I ought to let you know,' she finished rather lamely.

He actually laughed. Amanda was relieved, though she thought it a jolly funny reaction. 'Defending it from whom?' he said.

'Mr Bunting. He seized her in his arms and rained passionate kisses on her unwilling lips.'

'Where did you read that?'

'This week's *Teenager*. But it just fits, Daddy.'

He looked at her excited little face. He said, 'Are you trying to tell me you saw Mr Bunting kissing your mother?'

She nodded vigorously.

'Oh, Lord,' he said. He was no longer smiling.

He didn't want to know. If old Charles had

forgotten himself for a moment – well, he'd apologize to May who, no doubt, would accept the apology with her usual graciousness; then as soon as they were alone May would tell him, her husband, the whole story. And he, Jocelyn, would be very understanding, and they would probably finish up having a rather rueful laugh about it. But if he was put in the position of having to acknowledge publicly that he knew about it, it was going to be horribly embarrassing for everybody.

'Right ho, Mandy,' he said hopefully. 'I'll have a word with Mr Bunting sometime. I'm quite sure there's a perfectly simple explanation.'

But when you have a daughter like Amanda, you are not allowed to evade your moral responsibilities in this way. She was actually tugging at his arm, now. 'Daddy, you *must* come. Or it may be too late.' Too late for what, she wasn't quite sure. But something.

There was that about Amanda which precluded cowardice, or shirking of duty, or even the more socially acceptable forms of dishonesty. He went with her, down the stairs, across the hall, dragging his feet, Amanda tugging eagerly at his hand, across the living room towards the French windows. For Jocelyn, to walk towards an emotional scene in which he was certain to be involved, was rather like walking towards the block.

126

They reached the French window. Amanda opened it eagerly for her father, and stood aside for him to go through.

He made his reluctant entrance on to the lawn.

May was sitting in a wicker chair. She looked relaxed and serene. She was reading. A few yards away Charles Bunting was putting paint on canvas with swift, assured strokes. Neither of them saw Jocelyn.

Jocelyn stepped quietly and thankfully back into the living room. He looked hard at his daughter. 'I suppose,' he said, 'this wasn't a ploy to escape from your room?'

She fixed him with a stare that almost seared. 'Sorry, Amanda,' he muttered. And now he began to worry about his young daughter's emotional reaction. What mattered was not *what* she'd seen, but what she *thought* she'd seen. He didn't want any traumas. Oh, dammit, he *was* involved. He put an arm about her shoulder as they strolled back across the living room. He said, 'I don't think you need *worry* about this Amanda. You see, grown ups often kiss. Why, Mr Bunting always kisses Mummy when he says goodbye.'

'Not like this he doesn't,' said Amanda.

They walked on in silence, Jocelyn racking his brains for a further contribution. Amanda was wrapped in her own thoughts. At last: 'Will you call him out?' she asked. 'If you do, I should have pistols. There's a super spot on No Man's Heath.'

Jocelyn laughed. 'My dear child, there's nothing like that. Mr Bunting's a great friend of mine. I know he wouldn't do anything I wouldn't approve of.'

'*You* didn't see him kissing Mummy,' said Amanda.

Jocelyn was silent. And for the first time he felt a curious little stab. Not physical, yet unpleasantly sharp. If Amanda's highly coloured version was true, it didn't seem right for May to have been sitting there reading a magazine just now. She'd taken it jolly calmly. It was almost, he thought, as though she and Charles had been putting on an appearance of innocence for his benefit. He said, 'Right, Amanda. I must go and get on with some work.' He looked at her anxiously, wondering why he felt so helpless. And suddenly he knew. This was the first time he hadn't been able to fall back on May in a crisis involving the children. He said, 'Now you promise? You won't worry about this, will you, Mandy. It's nothing really.'

'Worry?' said Amanda. There were often times when she didn't understand her father. 'Worry? I think it's *super*.' And she hurried off like a reporter, who has just seen smoke pouring from the front windows of Buckingham Palace, in search of a tele-phone. 'Oh, bad shot, Gaylord,' she cried as she approached the tennis court.

'You put me off,' grumbled Gaylord, who had skied a ball into the paddock.

Roger and Christine went and slapped the net with their rackets while they chatted. Gaylord and Liz left the court to look for it. 'Hello Mandy,' said Liz, with as near an approach to a smile as could be expected from someone with a bleeding heart (Gaylord was being *ever* so friendly. But she didn't want friendship. She wanted *love*).

Mandy helped them search. She saw the ball almost immediately, but managed to heel it under a tussock. There were more important things than tennis, at the moment. 'I say, did you see all the excitement?' she asked.

'What excitement?' asked Gaylord, with as much interest as could be expected from someone else with a bleeding heart.

'Mr Bunting kissed Mummy on the lawn. *Passionately!*' said Amanda.

'Ah, here it is,' said Gaylord. 'Now where were we? Thirty-forty?'

'That's right.' said Liz whose bleeding heart Amanda's words had now filled with alarm. But she didn't want to know. Not now. If her father had made a nuisance of himself with her adored Mrs Pentecost (and she knew it was possible) she'd know soon enough. 'Your service,' she said.

Amanda went to see her grandfather, who greeted her without enthusiasm. She flopped down in the deck chair next to his. 'Did I wake you up?'

'Of course you didn't. I never sleep in the daytime. Effete habit.'

'Then if you weren't asleep,' Amanda said cosily, sliding down in her deck chair, 'I bet you saw Mr Bunting and Mummy locked in a fond embrace.'

'I saw nothing of the kind.'

'Then you must have been asleep. Because they were, right in the middle of the lawn, and from here–'

'I must have been reading the paper.'

'You weren't. 'Cos I was up at my bedroom window, escaping. And I saw *everything*, before I went to fetch Daddy. You weren't reading, Grandpa. But I couldn't see whether you had your eyes shut.'

'I do rest them occasionally. When you get to my age– You – fetched your father? What *is* all this?'

So she'd got a reaction at last. She told him.

When she'd gone he sat for a long time, thinking.

He wasn't surprised, frankly, for he was a shrewd old man, and saw far more of what went on than most people gave him credit for. And something had wakened him – someone shooting in the wood, perhaps – just in time to see Charles and May say a few apparently furious words to each other in the middle of the lawn before May sat down and took up her magazine, and Charles strode across and seized his palette.

No. He wouldn't be surprised. Bunting was a strange, hungry, lonely creature; and an artist to boot.

But May? John Pentecost yielded to no one in his admiration of May. A fine woman in every respect. Nevertheless, she was human, still young enough to have hot blood in her veins, yet old enough to heed the 'youth's a stuff will not endure' siren call. A woman of spirit, who might well respond to a spirited creature like Bunting. Especially with young Jocelyn shutting himself in his study day after day. Of course, one of the qualities he most admired in his daughter-in-law was her loyalty. She'd never do anything to hurt Jocelyn, he felt sure of that. Nevertheless, he hadn't lived as long as he had without learning that no human being is wholly predictable. He'd have a quiet word with Jocelyn, he decided. Remind him not to take May for granted. Tactful, of course. But then if anybody knew how to be tactful, he did. It was a gift for which he was humbly thankful. In fact, knowing how prickly other people could be, he didn't quite know how he'd have got through life without it.

Jocelyn, leaving off for a moment from sorting out his fictional characters' troubles, reached across and wrote in his desk diary: 'See Erl King's D.' In some way which he found it quite impossible to disentangle, the whole question of this girl's immediate future seemed to have landed in his court. He desperately wished it hadn't because it meant he had to think about it and he didn't want to think about anything except his fiction. Most particularly did he not want to think about this nonsense of Amanda's. Yet he could think of nothing else. He even made a diary note: 'See M re C.' But then he crossed it out. If there *had* been anything, which he very much doubted, May would be bursting in to tell him the moment the portrait painting session was over. Besides, he knew in his heart, he didn't need a diary note to remind him.

Nearly five o'clock. They were having a long session. He left his study, strolled into one of the bedrooms that overlooked the lawn.

The lawn was empty: no May, no Charles, no chair or easel or palette.

He was taken aback. There was something slightly sinister about that empty lawn.

He went back to his study. But he couldn't write. He was listening for his wife's footsteps on the stairs. She usually brought him a cup of tea about this time. That was when she would tell him.

He heard the chink of teacups, a woman's

footsteps. He found, to his surprise, that his hand was trembling.

The door opened. He braced himself. It was his wife, complete with a tray of tea.

She was bright, cheerful. But there *were* occasions when May could be too bright and too cheerful. When the brightness became brittle.

So it was, now. Once again he braced himself. 'Had a nice afternoon?'

'*Very* nice. You can't think how gorgeous it is, *having* to do nothing. It means your conscience can have an afternoon off, too.'

Did it, he wondered. He waited. Now she had picked up a draft letter he had written in longhand. 'You want this typing?' she asked.

'Some time. It's not urgent. In fact, if you'd like me to get Christine on it–? She did the other very well.'

She stood, looking at him thoughtfully. 'You *can* be wet at times,' she said.

'Me? Why?' Secretly, he was hurt, and alarmed.

'Oh, I don't know.' She gave him a sudden grin. 'Sorry, darling.'

To her surprise, he did not respond. He looked hard, and hostile. And his voice had a cold edge to it that she knew, but seldom heard. '*Why* am I wet at times?' He sat, watching her. 'Come on. I want to know.'

She said, trying to jolly him along. '*Darling!* I only meant – I've typed everything you've

133

ever written. Not very well, I know. But – it's been a labour of love. And – I don't think you need offer to put me out to grass the *moment* a new young filly appears on the scene.'

He refused to be jollied. 'I will *not* be called wet, May.'

She said miserably, 'Oh, I'm sorry, love.'

Now was the time, he knew, to have it out. *What's all this I hear about you and Charles?* The cards were in his hand. He could be angry, suspicious, accusing even. His position was unassailable.

But he hadn't the resolution. Or, frankly, the desire. He said, 'Sorry, old girl. It wasn't very tactful of me, was it.'

'That's all right.'

Now he yearned to be friendly. 'I'm glad it was such a lovely afternoon for you,' he said.

'Mmm.' She was reading the letter now.

Oh, why didn't she say something? 'And nothing untoward happened?' he asked. His mouth was dry.

'No, don't think so.' Her voice was quick and sharp. She was still reading the long letter. 'Oh, yes, I'd forgotten.' She went on reading.

'It did?' He grasped the edge of his desk, to stop his hand trembling.

She nodded, tossed the letter back into his tray. 'Good letter, that. *I'd* have been a bit more forthright. But that's me. Yes. Nine out of ten.'

'Thanks. Er – what happened untoward?'

'Your father was stung by a wasp. I gave him the full treatment, short of hospitalization.' She grinned down at him, knowing how much he hated such monstrous jargon.

'Poor Father,' he said absently. 'Er – is Charles still here?'

'No. He's beetled off. I say, the portrait's interesting. Not a bit like Mona Lisa. More like *Sunset Over Cardigan Bay* at the moment. But no doubt it will take shape.'

'Is Charles pleased with it?'

'I shouldn't think so, but you know Charles. Must go. Good letter, that.' She leaned over, pecked his forehead. 'And, Jocelyn?'

'Yes?'

'You're *not* wet, love.'

He sat on. Amanda, that little devil, *must* have made it up. It wasn't like her, he had to admit. Downright lying, even to save her own skin, wasn't her forte. And being mistaken certainly wasn't. Amanda saw the human comedy with far too clear an eye to make mistakes and May *had* been very brittle. Well, no doubt May would tell him about it in her own good time. If there was anything to tell. But he did wish she'd hurry up. Not that he was really suspicious or jealous, of course. Such a thing was unthinkable between him and May...

The study door opened. His father came in.

This was a most unusual honour. John Pentecost seldom visited his son's workroom because he did not, quite frankly, approve of his son's choice of livelihood. Scribblers he ranked only slightly above pop singers, unless of course they wrote rattling good yarns like Rider Haggard or that Hornblower chap, which Jocelyn obviously didn't. (Not that he'd read any of Jocelyn's books. But you'd only got to look at Jocelyn.)

'Hello, Father,' said Jocelyn.

The old man lowered himself into a chair, looked round him. 'Never understand what you want with all these books. Thought you wrote 'em, not read 'em.'

'One needs to know what other people have made of the human condition,' Jocelyn said, realizing he sounded pompous but not really caring. He was too busy wondering what brought his father here and whether it could possibly have anything to do with Amanda's story.

For perhaps the first time in his life the old man gave his mind to the creative process. 'I see,' he said at last. 'You read all this stuff, chew it over, and then regurgitate it in your own words, as it were.'

'Certainly not,' Jocelyn said, stung, yet wondering in his own mind whether the old man hadn't hit the nail on the head.

'But that's not what I came for,' said John Pentecost. He pulled out his pipe. 'Mind if I smoke?'

The old man filled his pipe. 'It's not easy to say in a few words,' he said.

It *was* about May. Jocelyn waited. His father went through his pockets, one by one: two trouser, two jacket, four waistcoat. 'Got a match?' he said at last.

Jocelyn threw him the matches. 'It's about May,' said John Pentecost. He concentrated on lighting his pipe.

Jocelyn licked his dry lips. 'What about her?' His voice was a croak.

'Damn fine woman. I always feel honoured to have such a woman in the family.' He looked at his son severely.

'So do I,' Jocelyn said.

'Yes.' John Pentecost gave his son one of his rare smiles. 'I think you do, Jocelyn. Only thing is–' he went through his pockets again – 'got a pipe cleaner?'

'Here you are.'

'Thanks.' The old man began a series of plumbing operations.

Jocelyn said, 'You were saying, the only thing is–?'

'Was I?'

'Yes.'

'What about?'

'May.'

'Oh yes. The only thing is, it's very easy to

137

start taking a woman like that for granted. Shutting yourself up in here, day after day, while she toils away below. Women need to have a bit of notice taken of them, you know. Oh, well, I'll be off. Hope you didn't mind my speaking frankly.' He heaved himself out of his chair.

'But you *haven't* spoken frankly,' cried Jocelyn. 'What's it all about, Father?'

'It's not about anything, dammit. I suppose I can think aloud without–?'

Jocelyn said: 'Father, it must be five years since you came into this room. Are you telling me that you came all the way up here simply to think aloud? Or were you out of matches and pipe cleaners?' he asked crossly.

'Well, since you ask,' said John Pentecost. 'That painter fellow. Not suggesting he's after any hanky panky, mind. But – well, a nod's as good as a wink to a blind horse, eh?'

Jocelyn said, in measured terms, 'Father, are you *daring* to suggest that May would allow Charles Bunting to make advances behind my back? Why, she'd blast him out of the water.'

''Course she would, dear boy.' He put a kindly hand on Jocelyn's shoulder, squeezed. 'Don't you give it another thought, Jocelyn.' He departed, well pleased with his mission. Said just enough to make Jocelyn think, without alarming him, he told himself.

The tennis party broke up. 'Thanks, Pentecost,' Roger Miles called as he went off with Christine to get his bicycle. They made a handsome couple.

'So long, Miles,' said Gaylord. He watched them go. Liz watched him watching them go. And saw longing and pain and hurt in his face and knew just how he felt, since she herself was feeling exactly the same. Being Liz, her yearning to comfort was even greater than her yearning to be comforted. To have slipped her hand into his, to say, 'Don't worry, love. The world is wide, there are plenty of fish in *English* waters and as a last resort there's even me–' this would have been wonderful. But she knew it would be no use. When a boy's eyes are on the moon, he does not see the clustering stars, still less the lamplight in the cottage window.

They were out of sight, now. Gaylord was able to give his attention to Liz. 'I say, she didn't half improve your tennis, Liz.'

'Do you think so?'

'Rather! You were serving quite well by the end of the afternoon. But she's terrific, isn't she?'

'Terrific,' said Liz.

'I thought it was jolly nice of her, helping you like that.'

'Yes.'

'I wish I could persuade her to stay.'

'Yes.'

139

'But it isn't only her. Mum doesn't want her to stay, either.'

She's not the only one, thought Liz. She grasped the handlebars of her bike. 'Thanks for the tennis, Gaylord.'

'That's all right. I say, if Christine *should* stay, you must come for another lesson.'

She cycled home through the late afternoon sunshine, sick at heart. She had had a humiliating afternoon. Oh, the German girl had been kind and patient, she couldn't have been friendlier. But to have one's shortcomings analysed and corrected in front of one's beloved, by *his* beloved – any farmyard hen at the bottom of the pecking order would have known exactly how Liz felt, that summer afternoon.

But it wasn't only that. There was, behind her heartache, another ominous shadow: the question of what her father had been up to.

What had Amanda said? 'Mr Bunting kissed Mrs Pentecost. *Passionately!*'

To Liz, the Pentecosts' friendship was vital. And not only because she loved Gaylord. To be accepted into this easy-going family, who never underrated the seriousness of life yet could treat it with the mockery it deserved – this was her only escape from loneliness, a brisk corrective to her own rather serious nature. To sit chatting with Mrs Pentecost, anything from clothes to a real heart to heart; to return Jocelyn's low friendly smile, to bask in Amanda's admiration, above all to be Gaylord's slave and handmaiden when he would let her: all this was her heaven. Surely, *surely* Father could not have risked spoiling all that for her!

The Rolls was in the drive. She went indoors. Silence. 'Anyone in?' she called. 'Here,' Came in a growl from his studio. She went in. He was subjecting a canvas to his usual vicious attack, did not look up. 'Don't interrupt,' he said. 'Go away.'

It was a perfectly normal greeting, and she quite understood. Artists had to be allowed to exercise their demons at their own time. But for once she didn't go away. She said, 'I want to talk to you, Father.'

'And I don't want to talk to you. Hop it.'

This wasn't normal behaviour. Normally he would have advanced on her glowering, seized her by the shoulders, bundled her out, and slammed the door on her with his sudden, disarming grin. She said, 'I think it was *horrible*.'

'What?' He went on with his demoniacal attack.

'*Did* you kiss poor Mrs Pentecost?'

For the first time he looked at her. 'Of *course* I kissed her. Infuriating woman, up and down like a blasted yo-yo. And my God this portrait means a lot to me. So I grabbed her shoulders to shove her down in her chair

141

and the next thing I knew I was kissing her. It's what's called a reflex action,' he explained.

'Oh, Daddy,' said Liz.

'*And* we'll have less of the poor Mrs Pentecost. That woman gave me a clout that would have felled an ox.'

'Oh, Daddy,' said Liz. And began to cry, with the quiet sadness of a wet April evening.

He was appalled. He dropped his palette, swept a couple of frames and a canvas from a chair, and with clumsy arms about her, sat her down. 'Liz! What is it? Young Gaylord been upsetting you?'

She even managed a little smile. She shook her head. 'It's not Gaylord. It's you. What's Mr Pentecost going to say?'

'Old Jocelyn? He's not one to make mountains out of molehills. We're old friends.'

'That's what I mean,' she said quietly.

'Oh, Lord,' he said. 'It's strange,' he said. 'How one forgets. Innocence. The bright world of innocence. And the world's slow stain.' He cleared another chair, sat down beside her. 'Shall I tell you what happened afterwards?'

She nodded, wiping her eyes.

'I went on painting her. And after a time she said, "I shall have to tell Jocelyn, you know," and I said, "Yes, I realized you would." And I went on painting. A bit later she said, "Does this mean I'm going to be assaulted every time I'm alone with you?" and I said, "It does not, Scouts' honour, and I think it would be truer to say you assaulted me." Then I did quite useful work. And at last I said, "But the fact does remain that I'm in love with you, May, and I'm a desperately lonely man, and if I thought there was any possibility of your leaving Jocelyn for me I should badger you night and day, but I know you and he are still besotted with each other and frankly I can't blame you, so I might as well save my breath to cool my porridge." And May said, "Good. Frankly, Charles, I'm glad this has been said, and now we know where we are, and I'm flattered and honoured that you say that you love me and I hope we can go on being friends without any more nonsense.'" He put his hand on her knee. 'So you see, little one, to us old worldlings it isn't as earth-shattering as it seems to you.'

'I still wish you hadn't,' she said. 'It – spoils things.'

'I'm sorry,' he said quietly.

Suddenly she grinned at him. 'Poor old Dad. Isn't it *rotten*, loving someone who doesn't love you?'

'Rotten,' he said. He too grinned. 'But not quite as rotten at forty as at seventeen.'

'I vote we have a meal soon,' said Liz. 'I didn't have a very big lunch.'

'Yes. Mustn't be late. I've arranged to go and do a bit more to the portrait after supper.'

CHAPTER 10

Amanda did not let the excitement over Mummy and Mr Bunting stop her posting her letter. She did have a few moments doubt when she discovered that the cost of the stamp would have bought quite a few of the sweets on sale in the Shepherd's Warning Post Office. But she was not one to be deflected easily from her purpose, and the sound of the letter dropping into the box filled her with both excitement and alarm.

And, as the days passed, her alarm increased. If Christine got a letter or a telegram from her mother, sooner or later questions were going to be asked. And Amanda knew that once questions started being asked they always quickly focused on her. She had no idea how long post took to and from Germany. But she awaited the daily arrival of the postman with trepidation.

Nearly a week passed, however. Christine helped May, and said nothing about returning home. Roger Miles appeared and disappeared, and Christine treated him and

Gaylord with equal pleasantness, equal amused aloofness. Amanda felt like someone who has lit a long slow fuse, knowing that at the end of the fuse stands an enormous barrel of gunpowder. And May and Jocelyn both felt that a piece of grit (neither of them would have admitted to thinking it more than that) had got into the smooth machinery of their marriage.

May was most unhappy. Charles had kissed her, it was nothing. Or would have been nothing if she'd mentioned it to Jocelyn straight away. But some quirk in her make-up had prevented her. Why? Was this something she wanted to keep in her heart, that she did not want to share even with Jocelyn? Was it the feeling that she was his, absolutely, mind and body, and that this one thing she wanted for herself, like a nun, hiding some worthless trinket inside her habit, to call Mine! She did not know. She only knew that she had not been able to tell him, and that every day that passed made it more impossible. And that until it was told it would be there, between them, even though Jocelyn never did hear about it.

One afternoon of thunder heat, of climbing cumuli and hot, coppery sunlight, and baked grass, she said, 'Jocelyn, the summer's nearly gone. Come and sit with me for once, under the elms.'

He smiled wistfully, apologetically. 'Sorry,

May. I *must* get this finished.'

'Of course,' she said. She wandered out, to the parched shade beneath the elms where stood two garden chairs. She flopped into one of them, closed her eyes. The heat was intense, airless. The flow of her thoughts became erratic, images flickered absurdly before her closed eyes. She slept.

The sound of someone sitting down in the next chair did not rouse her. And when a male voice said, 'Going to be a storm,' she did not open her eyes, but smiled sweetly and said, 'Darling, you came after all.'

The voice said bitterly, 'It isn't your darling Jocelyn. It's only old Charles.'

She sat up, stared at him fearfully. He said, 'That smile, when you were still asleep and thought you heard your husband's voice. It was – ineffable.'

She went on staring. He said, 'If I could paint that smile, and call it *"Love,"* or *"Welcome,"* it would be in every Boots branch in the land, as well as in the Tate. But I couldn't. Rembrandt couldn't. Only God.'

'Did – *did* I smile?' she was still confused.

'Like an angel. And that's not just a cliché. I tell you, May, I'd sell my soul to the Devil for a woman who'd smile at me like that.'

Impulsively she put out her hand. He pressed it to his lips with both of his. And held it there.

She was still drowsy. She made a half-hearted attempt to pull her hand away, but it was too hot and she was too sleepy. She sat there, eyes half closed. Beneath her the coconut-matting grass, all about her the hot stillness of the summer afternoon, above her the green, secret places of the high elms. Her mind was still hung with cobwebs of sleep, her body limp and soft with the summer's heat, her will run down like the spring of an unwound clock. And Charles was gazing at her with an expression that would normally have disturbed her considerably.

She *must* make an effort of will.

She couldn't. They stayed there, like statues, on a tomb, silent, unmoving, and she was afraid. It was as though they, together with the whole countryside, were charmed into immobility. Yet an immobility that must soon snap like an overstretched fiddle string.

Then something very frightening happened. A sudden clatter in the high elms shattered the silence of the afternoon. It continued, growing nearer. Then a large bird fell out of the tree, and landed almost at May's feet.

May screamed, and jumped to her feet.

The bird lay for a moment scrabbling at the dry grass. Then it reared up, spreading its wings. It lifted its beak towards the green, secret places that had been its home. Then it fell back, and did not move again.

Charles examined it. 'Wood pigeon,' he

147

said. 'Dead. But not a mark on it. Extra-ordinary thing to happen.'

'Yes,' said May. 'Poor thing.' But pity was the least of her emotions. Horror, at this sudden eruption of death into her comfortable world. Fear, at this creature of the wild suddenly joining his life to hers, forcing himself on her in the very moment of death.

Charles said, 'Isn't he *beautiful!* Look at those colours, how wonderfully they blend, look at the sleekness of that head, the pity of those dead eyes.'

But May, shuddering, scarce able to breathe, would not, *dare* not, look. The bird had risen up, wings outspread, beak lifted, proud. But death had wasted no time. In the moment of striving, in the moment of pride, it had struck. An omen? She did not know of what. She only knew that every nerve in her body was quivering with horror, revulsion, shame. That the walls of her civilization were down. She was one with the small, helpless creatures of the wild. Why should Mrs Jocelyn Pentecost vaunt herself more than a wood pigeon, dying on a hot, September day?

Jocelyn, too, was most unhappy. The green-eyed monster was gnawing at his vitals. It was a ridiculous situation. He'd only got to ask May, frankly, what if anything had happened. But he wasn't going to be the first to broach the subject. And as the days passed, and she

148

said nothing, he grew more and more morose and irritable. And that evening, as he sat alone in his study, he came to a decision. He *had* to know. If May said nothing this evening, he'd jolly well ask her what had happened between her and Charles.

Nothing had happened, he told himself. If it had, May would have told him as soon as she saw him. Few women, and certainly not his dear May, had ever latched on to the concept of actually thinking before they spoke. Besides, a secret between him and May was unthinkable.

And yet–? May had certainly been on edge. He *couldn't* put it out of his mind. Dammit, he could no more put it out of his mind than he could have put a raging tooth out of his mind.

That little stabbing pain was still there, and it was no longer so little. It was a constant ache. It wasn't jealousy, of course. *He* – a civilized, reasonably well-educated, twentieth century man, whose id and ego were kept tuned and balanced like twin carburettors – he'd very soon know if he were suffering from a crude emotion like jealousy. *And* would give himself very short shrift. No. It wasn't jealousy. It was just that a chap – dammit to hell, old Charles must be an absolute swine!

May spoke on the inside telephone, 'Jocelyn! Supper in ten minutes.'

'Bring me up a tray, May,' he said. 'I can't

leave off now.'

Ten minutes later there were footsteps on the stairs. This was just about the bit where Othello asked to borrow her handkerchief, he thought. Then he thought: that's the worst of being a literary gent. You see everything through the Bard's eyes. And before you know where you are you're Othello, or Lear, or Hamlet, and your little problem has been blown out of all recognition. Simmer down, Pentecost! And he waited, a little more relaxed, to have a friendly chat with that dear companion his wife about what if anything had been going on.

The door opened. Christine Haldt tiptoed in, set a tray down on his desk, and began to tiptoe out again.

He said, 'I'm not asleep, you know.'

She said, 'Of course. I know you will not be asleep when you are working. But I do not want to disturb the flow of ideas.'

The only flow of ideas this afternoon, he thought, had been out of the window. And now he remembered that he was supposed to be organizing this girl's future. He said, 'Are you still thinking of going back to Germany, Christine?'

'Perhaps I do not go just yet,' she said. 'Roger Miles wishes to play more tennis. Also he has an uncle with riding stables.'

'I see,' said Jocelyn, wondering whether this meant he ought to see the Department of Employment and Miss Ferris, or just pretend he hadn't asked.

He chose the last course. 'Where's Mrs Pentecost?' he said, oh so casually.

'I think she is not organized. She says the hot weather has made her sleepy. But it is *my* belief,' said Christine darkly, 'that she is still upset by the unwelcome attentions.'

'What unwelcome attentions?' asked Jocelyn, giving up all attempts to sound casual. But at that moment May said on the intercom: 'Stop chatting up Christine, darling, and tell her her soup's getting cold.'

'May,' he said urgently, 'can you come up for a moment?'

'In the middle of supper, dear? Won't it keep?'

'Yes,' he said. 'It'll keep.' He said to Christine. 'Your soup's getting cold.'

'So.' She turned in the doorway. 'My Aunt Ulrike was paid unwelcome attentions by a Herr Baron, much to the distress of my Onkel Willi.'

'Your family seem to have had some interesting experiences,' he said. She went.

What could he do but wait? Having asked for a tray to be sent up, he couldn't barge in in the middle of supper. And even if he did he couldn't ask May in front of the whole intrigued family what Charles had been up to. He could only wait – calm, unemotional, detached, as befitted a civilized, twentieth century human being. But who did old Charles thinks he was, driving up here in his Rolls and kissing Jocelyn's wife? It was nothing to get worked up about, of course. But he had to admit he didn't like it.

He toyed with his food. The house was silent. He waited. Eventually he would hear the dining room door open, the sudden buzz of cheerful conversation, the clatter of dishes, announcing that supper was over. And then – his wife's footsteps on the stairs.

Once, in the distance, he thought he heard the slam of a car door, and a few seconds' murmur of conversation; then silence again. Supper was taking a long time! But then, at last, he heard the sounds he had been waiting for – the cheerful breaking up of the supper party.

He waited.

No footsteps on the stairs. She must have decided to wash the supper things first. He really did begin to feel a little put out. Anything May did was right, of course, must be right. But he'd got to get to the bottom of this tonight. And it would be *so* much easier if May brought up the subject.

There was only one consolation. In a marriage, however happy, there is a constant jockeying for position. And in this Jocelyn never stood a chance. May could outmanoeuvre him every time. But on this occasion, he told himself, May had played her cards wrong. Her delay meant that when she did tell him he would be able to be understanding, forgiving, and even faintly amused. It would be an unusual experience for him.

The sudden thought that perhaps she'd no intention of telling him struck him like a blow. After all, old Charles probably was attractive to women. And he *was* somebody; not that that would attract May, of course.

What had his father said? 'Shutting yourself in up here, day after day–?' Jocelyn felt a cold sweat on his brow. The tray – that was a good excuse. 'Thought you'd like to get these things washed up, old girl.' He picked it up, hurried downstairs with it, barged into the kitchen, said, 'Oh Lord. Sorry. *Sorry*,' and barged back into the hall where Amanda found him clutching the tray and looking bewildered. 'I know,' she said with great understanding. 'Gaylord and the Rhine Maiden in the kitchen, and Mummy and Mr Bunting in the living room. If you're like me you're beginning to feel shut out.'

Amanda's summary of the situation was basically correct. Charles Bunting had arrived just as they were finishing supper, demanding that May go and be painted. Christine had offered to see to everything, Gaylord had offered to help her (washing up wasn't his idea of heaven, but washing up alone with Christine was). Amanda had offered to help Gaylord and Christine, and had been rebuffed. So had her offer to help Mr Bunting mix his paints.

So Christine had washed up and Gaylord had dried and put away. And Gaylord, seeing that loved head bowed over the sink, and the light falling on that cascade of hair, said in a strangled voice, 'You're very beautiful, Christine,' and Christine had smiled at him over her shoulder and said modestly, 'I do not think I am yet sufficiently mature to be called beautiful. Pretty, yes. But not yet beautiful.'

'Well, *I* think you are,' said Gaylord, drying plates and going very red.

After a time he said, 'Christine?'

'Yes.'

'I would like to kiss you.'

Christine went and dried her hands on the towel. 'So,' she said. 'Just one.'

Gaylord walked slowly towards her. He looked at that sunburnt loveliness of cheek, the wonder of those eyes, the softness of those parted lips. The thought that in a moment he would touch them with *his* lips, that her scented breath would mingle with his, that the fragrance of her hair would be in his nostrils – this was almost too much for him. Clumsily he put his arms about her. Clumsily he kissed her smiling lips. And it was all as wonderful and beautiful as he had imagined. Christine was soft, and scented, and sweet as a berry. But she was more, far more, than the sum of these things. To a boy brought up in the monasticism of an English public school she was a creature from another world, half splendidly human, half divine. Suddenly he knew what life was about. What was cricket, even a hard game of rugger, compared with this ecstasy of kissing?

'That is enough,' she said.

'One more?' he pleaded.

'Very well. But only one.'

He looked into her smiling face; discovering, for the first time, the wonder and mystery and loveliness in the eyes of the young beloved. His lips yearned again towards hers. She kissed him long and lovingly. For the first time he saw in the girl's eyes the ardent brooding look of love. 'You are only a boy,' she murmured. 'But – a sweet boy, and it is sweet to kiss you.'

'I love you,' he said in a choked voice. 'You won't go, will you, Christine?'

'No. I will stay. As long as your mother will let me.' She smiled at him fondly and tenderly.

It was then that a voice in the doorway said, 'Oh Lord. Sorry. *Sorry.*'

Gaylord, in his present highly nervous and transported state, almost leapt in the air. And Christine returned to the sink. 'It was the Father,' she said. 'It is unbecoming that such dalliance should be observed by the Father. He will think me a not very earnest au pair, and will send me packing.'

'You did say last week you *wanted* to go home,' said Gaylord, coming behind her, putting his hands on her shoulders, turning her round to face him. He swallowed. With a dry mouth he asked hopefully, 'Don't you want to any more?'

'Not any more,' she said. And, with a sudden change of subject Gaylord found slightly bewildering, 'It appears that the riding stables of the uncle of Roger Miles are unusually elegant for the English Midlands.'

Amanda was quite right. Jocelyn *was* beginning to feel shut out. And this filled him with a, for him, most unusual resentment. He was angry with everybody, it seemed, and with the whole situation: Gaylord kissing au pairs in the kitchen (and this sight had taken him back twenty-five years to the torments and ecstasies and follies of *his* first love; O, pale hands of Doreen Wilkinson, where are you now, who lies beneath your spell? Doreen Wilkinson! She'd married a half back, Richards, and gone to live in Swindon. And he remembered, with shame and incredulity, how he and Richards had once fought over her, on a distant summer's evening. He could still remember the smell of dry earth and trampled grass, and the hot, salt taste of a torn lip; and, worse than either, the shame of inglorious defeat). His father toiling up to his study to do a woolly-minded Iago act, May behaving in a manner that seemed, on the face of it, disloyal. There he'd been, toiling away in his sunless study throughout one of the loveliest weeks of the year, toiling away in order to keep May and the rest of them in the comfort to which they were accustomed; and what had *they* been doing? Enjoying the sunshine, kissing away the golden summer hours.

In anyone else he would have recognized the symptoms: self-pity and jealousy. But he regarded self-pity as one of the most de- structive of human emotions, so it was pretty obvious he himself would never give way to it. As for jealousy – the idea of him being jealous about May was simply laughable.

But he wasn't spending the evening in the hall, just so that Charles and May could have the living room to themselves. Normally he would have been only too pleased to sit in his study. But this evening he was too restless even for work. He put his hand on the knob of the living room door. 'Going in?' said Amanda. 'I most certainly am,' said Jocelyn. 'Whoopee,' said Amanda. 'I'm coming with you.'

May was sitting in her usual chair, reading a magazine. Charles had set up his easel a few feet away. The French windows were open to the evening. Just outside the windows John Pentecost smoked a cigar and mulled over his conversation with young Jocelyn. Jocelyn hadn't apparently taken much notice. Nevertheless, the old man decided he'd played his cards absolutely right. Tactful, fatherly, restrained – it had been a masterful effort.

Out of the corner of her eye May saw someone enter the room. She turned slightly. It was Jocelyn and Amanda. 'Hello, darlings,' she said. 'Charles will let you stay if you keep absolutely quiet.'

'Will you sit *still*, woman!' demanded Charles.

'Don't call my wife woman,' said Jocelyn.

Charles, May and Amanda looked at him in astonishment.

Charles said, 'Honestly, I'd rather paint a five-year-old child. Ever since I began this portrait I've been interrupted and harassed.' He flung down his palette. 'Do you realize–? I paint Lady Mayoresses at a thousand quid a go, and I get absolute discipline. They daren't move a muscle, poor old devils. But May–'

'Are you criticizing my wife?' Jocelyn asked in a quiet but furious voice.

'Yes I am. I think I deserve a little co-operation. After all, some people would think it something of an honour.'

Jocelyn walked across to Charles and punched him on the nose.

What was perhaps even most astonishing of this extraordinary behaviour was the fact that Jocelyn, for perhaps ten blissful seconds, felt rather pleased with himself. Especially since old Charles went backwards over a chair and finished up sprawled on the hearthrug, clutching his nose with both hands and moaning loudly. For a mild, scholarly man like Jocelyn to find that Cave Man Pentecost, whose very existence he had always secretly doubted, was alive and well and living much nearer the surface than expected, was heady wine indeed.

But despite Amanda's clasped hands, shining eyes, and cry of 'Oh, Daddy, that was *super*,' the mood dissolved almost before it had begun, to be replaced by an appalled awareness of what he had done.

And there was his dear May, helping Charles into a chair, trying to staunch the flow of blood, and giving Jocelyn a look that mingled contempt, anger and fears for his sanity in equal proportions. And here came his father in through the French windows, demanding to know what had happened, and giving it as his firm opinion that if Charles had got a nosebleed it was through being out in the hot sun all afternoon, he'd thought at the time it was asking for trouble.

May snapped, 'Don't just *stand* there, Jocelyn. Get a bowl of cold water, and a sponge.'

'Oh. Ah. Yes,' said Jocelyn, moving towards the door.

Amanda said, gleefully, 'It wasn't the hot sun, Grandpa. Daddy biffed him.'

John Pentecost took his cigar out of his mouth. He stared. 'I don't believe it,' he said at last.

'I don't see why you shouldn't,' said Jocelyn truculently from the doorway. 'Just because I don't normally throw my weight about.'

'But you can't say boo to a goose,' the old man pointed out reasonably.

'He said boo to this one. And how!' said Amanda, gazing worshipfully at her father.

'Don't say "And how",' said Jocelyn.

'Do you think it's broken?' said Charles.

'Oh, *I'll* get the sponge and bowl,' May said angrily. She paused to gaze anxiously at her patient. 'Will you be all right for a minute, Charles?'

Charles looked doubtful. John Pentecost said, 'Well, if this doesn't beat cockfighting.' He gazed at his son with a sort of reluctant admiration.

Suddenly the enormity of what he had done hit Jocelyn with tremendous force. He, a grown man, had behaved like a schoolboy! Could being reminded of that old humiliation over Doreen Wilkinson, coming on top of his anger and irritation, have taken him back twenty-five years?

The only possible thing left for him to do was grovel. He walked across to the chair where Charles sprawled. 'My dear chap,' he began.

To his amazement Charles held his crooked arm protectively across his face, gazed over it at Jocelyn with startled eyes, and cowered.

It was the first time in his whole life that anyone had cowered before Jocelyn. He found it an intoxicating experience. The temptation to make another threatening gesture was very strong. But his natural kindliness was even stronger. 'I really don't know what to say–' he began again.

May came in with the bowl, elbowed Jocelyn roughly out of her way, and began mopping up Charles.

'I'd never have believed it. Never,' said John Pentecost.

Gaylord and Christine came in. Christine looked cool and self-possessed. Gaylord looked flushed and a little wild, as though he had just passed through a shattering emotional experience, as indeed he had. He had only one ambition left in life: to kiss Christine again – as soon and as often as possible.

Amanda greeted them joyfully. When something exciting happened there were never enough people to tell. 'Gaylord! Daddy and Mr Bunting have been fighting over Mummy.'

'What nonsense!' said May. For once in her life she had the appearance of having lost control of a situation. It would hardly be putting it too strongly to say she looked flustered.

Gaylord said, 'I don't believe it.'

'My reaction precisely,' said his grandfather. He shook his head. 'But I'm afraid it's true, dear boy.'

Christine said, 'I am indeed glad that I did not return home earlier. Had I done so I should have taken away an entirely erroneous view of the English – and especially of Herr Pentecost.'

'There,' May said to Charles soothingly. 'Does that feel any better?'

'No,' said Charles.

'Well, the bleeding's stopped, anyway.'

'That's a fat lot of good if my nose is broken.'

'I don't think it *is* broken, Charles.'

'How the devil do *you* know? It *feels* broken.'

'Don't speak to May like that,' said Jocelyn, hearing his voice rising again. But this time Charles did not cower. He'd got May between him and Jocelyn.

Christine said, 'When I first come, I think Herr Pentecost is milk and water. But it is not so. First he deals firmly with the recalcitrant child–' (She got a look from Amanda that should have killed) – 'then he fights for his woman. So I cry, "Rule, Britannia. Britannia, rule the waves",' and taking the astonished Jocelyn's hand she kissed it respectfully.

'Hear, hear,' said Amanda, with equal fervour.

But May said, in a voice a mixture of ice and cold steel, 'Well, I'm glad someone approves of you, Jocelyn. Because I certainly don't.'

John Pentecost shook his head sagely. 'May's right, you know, Jocelyn. Can't go taking the law into our own hands, can we?'

'I'm *sure* it's broken,' moaned Charles.

'Well stop rubbing it,' snapped May.

There had been a time when Gaylord would have been as fascinated as Amanda by these adult shenanigans. Now however, he found them rather childish. There was no doubt about it. Suddenly, in the last hour even, he had matured. And he still had that idée fixe about kissing Christine. 'Come for a walk,' he murmured out of the side of his mouth. 'I'll see you outside the back door.'

She shook her head. 'No. Not now. I see you in the morning.'

'Please!' he begged.

'No!'

Somehow, one did not argue with Christine. The morning was aeons away. But it would come. 'Going out, Mum,' he called. 'Shan't be long.'

There was a part of May's brain that always recorded her family's exits and entrances. But so harassed was she at the moment that she didn't even hear Gaylord.

She was still rather helplessly holding the bowl of water and the sponge. The skirt and jumper she was wearing for her portrait were splashed with water and blood. And Christine was still gazing adoringly at Jocelyn, and Amanda was saying there was someone at the door, should she go and answer it, and Charles was saying lugubriously that he supposed he'd better drive home before his eyes closed up completely.

She concentrated on Charles. So Amanda took it upon herself to go and open the front door.

She was surprised to find a very beautiful lady on the step. The lady looked at Mandy with interest and – could it be? – amusement. 'Miss Amanda Pentecost?' she asked.

'Yes,' said Amanda, flattered but a little scared by this formal title.

'I believe you have written to me,' said the lady.

Amanda stared. 'But – you're not Mrs Haldt?'

'Why not?'

'Well, you're in England.'

'So I am. Thanks to your letter. I flew. Now. I believe you have my daughter.'

Amanda swallowed. This was not at all what she had bargained for. A letter would have been bad enough. But a whole German lady! 'I – I'll fetch her,' said Amanda.

'Thank you, my dear. But I think I ought to see your mother. There are certain questions, explanations.'

That was what Amanda was afraid of 'Perhaps you'd better come in,' she said unhappily.

'Thank you. It might be as well.'

Amanda went and opened the living-room door. But it was some time before she could make herself heard. May was saying, 'You're not driving yourself home in that state, Charles. Jocelyn will take you in our car.' Adding, nastily, 'It's the least he can do,' and Charles was saying, 'What? Let *him* drive me? I'd as soon sup with the Borgias, and anyway I shall need the Rolls in the morning, I've got an exhibition opening at the Ingerby *Swan*, and *everyone* will be asking whether I've gone four rounds with Muhammed Ali, I can just hear them.' And Jocelyn was looking hurt, and John Pentecost was asking anyone who'd listen whether *they* didn't think it beat cockfighting.

Suddenly everyone stopped talking and looked at the doorway. 'Christine's mum,' Amanda said simply. And wished that the floor would swallow her up.

'*Mutti!*' cried Christine. There followed what appeared to be a brisk exchange of fire between her and her mother in rapid German. Then Frau Haldt came into the room, smiling graciously at everyone except Christine.

She was one of those small, compact, reposeful women who glide as though on castors, and who never make a quick or unnecessary movement. She had her daughter's warm colouring. She looked round the room with great self-possession, and said, 'So. You must be Mrs Pentecost.'

'Yes,' said May, shoving the bowl of water down on an occasional table and holding her arm so that it covered the worst of the bloodstains. *'Do* sit down. This *is* a surprise.' It was, too.

'I imagined it might be, since my daughter led me to believe she was in the Harz Mountains. But–' She gave May a smile whose glint was not unlike that of moonlight on ice – 'You were not to know that, Mrs Pentecost.'

'I certainly did not.'

'No. Though, to be fair, your young daughter did.'

Here we go, thought Mandy. But Mrs Haldt went on, in the friendliest manner. *'You* simply accepted her without question. Not, I think, what we would have done in Germany. But then, our outlook is so different in many ways, is it not?'

May said, 'I did *not* accept her, with or without question. I was sending her back. But I was certainly giving her a few days to recover. In England,' she said acidly, 'we

166

temper ruthlessness with a little consideration.'

'Of course. My daughter put you in a very difficult position, Mrs Pentecost. Few of us like being put into a situation where we have to take decisive action.'

If there was one thing May prided herself on it was her capacity for decisive action. But now an enchanted John Pentecost was holding a chair for the lady with tremendous aplomb. She gave him a smile that made his senses reel, and sat down gracefully. The old man said, 'I'm afraid, madam, we've had a slight contretemps.'

'Just a little accident,' May said brusquely.

'Accident my foot,' said Charles, loud and clear. 'It was a brawl, Frau Haldt, a fracas. What's German for fracas?'

'*Ein Spektakel? Ein Aufruhr?*'

'Then we have had a *Spektakel*, or *Aufruhr*,' Charles said with relish. 'Christine's employer has just punched me on the nose.'

'Because he made passionate love to Mummy,' explained Amanda.

'I see,' said Frau Haldt.

There was then a silence. After which Frau Haldt said, 'So. It is interesting to see the English permissiveness at close-quarters. I had not realized it had spread to the middle class and the higher age brackets.'

'Permissiveness?' cried Charles. 'Permissiveness?' He pointed a dramatic finger at

May. 'I kiss an old and respected friend, almost *en passant*. And what happens? She sends me reeling. And then her husband, another old and dear friend, after brooding over it in silence for nearly a week, breaks my nose for me.' He rubbed it tenderly. 'Those two are about as permissive as a lioness and her mate.'

'I *didn't* break it,' said Jocelyn. 'It was a mere tap.'

'Of course it's broken. I can feel bones waggling about.'

'Come here,' said Frau Haldt. 'Kneel down.'

Charles, rather to his own, and certainly to everyone else's, surprise, went and knelt before her. And was suddenly transported. From this viewpoint she had the repose and beauty of a Leonardo Madonna. With cool, infinitely gentle fingers she felt the bridge of his nose. 'It's not broken,' she said at last. 'You will not lose your beauty, sir.'

May was interested to see whether he would be as ungracious with Frau Haldt as he had been with her. But no. He growled, 'It *feels* broken.' He struggled to his feet, gave her his hungry grin. 'Thank you, madam. It feels better already.' Then his manner changed. 'I'll be off,' he said brusquely.

'You're not going alone, Charles. Jocelyn will come with you.'

'How do I get back?' asked Jocelyn,

clutching wildly at a straw.

'You borrow Liz's bike,' said May, snatching the straw from his grasp.

Charles grunted. He collected his oils and brushes into a wooden case, draped a cloth over his canvas and put it under his arm.

Frau Haldt watched these preparations with great interest. Now she said, 'You are an artist, sir?'

'I try to be,' he said with unusual humility.

'Might a stranger ask to see your picture?'

He uncovered it, held it out to her.

Frau Haldt studied it keenly. Then she turned and studied May keenly. Then she returned to the picture. 'It is good,' she said. 'It flatters a little, but not too much. Yes. It is good.'

'Thank you,' said Charles, who was normally prickly over any comment on his work, resenting criticism and regarding praise as patronizing. He sounded as pleased as Punch.

Frau Haldt said, 'I should like to have seen more of your work. But alas, we are leaving tomorrow on the morning plane.'

'I am sorry,' Charles said simply. Gravely, he kissed her hand. 'So long, May,' he called. 'Thanks for acting as my second. Come on, Jocelyn.'

Jocelyn bowed to Frau Haldt, who inclined to him courteously, and followed Charles. Not only was he going to be subjected to

Charles' driving. A six-mile journey with someone you have just punched on the nose called for more social dexterity than Jocelyn thought himself capable of. He had only one consolation: he hadn't got to cope with the charming but formidable Frau Haldt. That was firmly in May's court; and by the time he'd cycled back whatever needed resolving ought to be resolved. Which, he realized miserably, meant that May would be free to express herself over the Spektakel, Aufruhr or fracas. And from what he had seen of her first reactions, what she had to express would not be complimentary. What a fool he was, he thought. A short time ago he had had every reason to feel aggrieved and injured. He had even been congratulating himself on a situation where he could be understanding, forgiving and faintly amused. He would have had his wife, if not actually apologizing, at least on the defensive. And *now* look who was on the defensive! May was going to tell him he'd behaved outrageously, and that she was thoroughly ashamed of him. And the devil of it was, she'd be quite right.

Charles switched on the ignition. The car began to move, edged past a waiting taxi in the drive, and a second later, it seemed to Jocelyn, the glowing speedometer showed seventy. Jocelyn said, 'I behaved irrationally.'

'So that's what you call it,' said Charles. The speed went up to eighty.

'It was an obvious case of atavism,' said Jocelyn.

Charles drove in silence.

'Once, when I was asleep,' said Jocelyn reminiscently, 'May turned over in bed and accidentally stuck her elbow in my mouth. And, do you know, I *bit* her. I can remember the feeling now: blind, animal fury.'

Charles drove on in silence.

Jocelyn said, 'In that moment, between sleeping and waking, I went back to Neanderthal man.'

Charles drove on in silence.

Jocelyn said, 'I actually growled, like a dog worrying a bone.'

'I'm lucky you didn't get me by the ankle, then. Well, that's not taken long. The bike's in the shed.'

Jocelyn climbed out of the car. 'I'm sorry, Charles,' he said pathetically.

'Oh, come in and have a drink,' said Charles. 'It'll do us both good.'

'Are you sure? I mean–?'

'Stop dithering, man.' He led the way into the studio, swept the clutter out of a couple of deep leather chairs. 'Sit down. Now. I'm having a large cognac. What about you?'

'I think I could do with the same.'

Charles poured the drinks. They sat back, long legs outstretched. Charles sighed deeply. 'Good. We haven't wakened Liz. Save a lot of explanations – tonight.'

They sipped in silence. Jocelyn looked at the romantic clutter of landscapes, nudes, Lady Mayoresses, easels, paints, palettes and frames; and thought, I suppose I was a bit stuffy, getting so worked up about a mere kiss between an artist and his sitter. He said, pointing, 'I like that one.'

'Which? The naked blonde? Yes. Interesting bone structure. Actually, she was a children's crossing warden in Leicester.'

'She must have looked very different on duty. But I really meant the seascape.'

'Skegness, dear boy, believe it or not. Here, let me top you up. Now then. Why did you punch me on the nose?'

'I'm sure it was atavism, Charles. I told you.'

'Atavism my left leg. It was because I kissed May.'

It was a pity, thought Jocelyn, that there was so much nonsense talked about drinking cognac. Swishing it round in the glass, savouring the bouquet. Sheer waste of time. To be really appreciated, he decided, it should be *swigged*. That way you got the full flavour. That way it was a fiery sword, Wagnerian in its power. 'Let me top you up,' said Charles.

He poured more brandy, lay back in his chair. He said, 'Do you know what I should do, if I were married to a sweet May, and another man kissed her?'

172

'No?'

'I should put on my climbing boots.' He took a long sip. 'Then I should knock him down and jump on him. Hard.'

He studied his friend thoughtfully. 'You *are* a bit feeble, you know, Jocelyn.'

'I suppose I am,' said Jocelyn.

'After all, dammit, a woman like May's worth putting up a show for.'

'Of course,' said Jocelyn.

'Still,' Charles said tolerantly, 'we're made differently. It just – doesn't do to be too easy going, old man.'

Jocelyn took another swig. In some way that he couldn't quite analyse, he seemed to have got himself edged on to the wrong side of this conversation.

'Let me top you up,' said Charles. 'Then I'll give you a couple of toasts.'

He topped them up. He lifted his glass. He said simply, 'To your adorable wife, my dear fellow.'

'Thank you,' murmured Jocelyn, deeply touched.

'And to your adorable visitor, the Erl King's Daughter's mother.'

'Is she adorable? I didn't get the impression May thought so.'

'My dear fellow, she's superb. She's got everything – beauty, poise, warmth, presence. But, like everyone else, married.' He sighed even more deeply. *'Sag mir wo die*

173

Mädchen sind.'

A shocked voice in the doorway cried, 'Daddy! Mr Pentecost! Why, whatever's happened?'

Liz, in a pink dressing gown, and with her hair in a plait about her right shoulder, and her face still soft from sleep, looked frightened and vulnerable and very, very young.

The two men rose, thereby giving Liz a clearer view of her father's face. 'Daddy! You're hurt. Was it the car?' The thing she was always dreading. Still, the way Daddy drove, if he'd really had an accident and got away with a slightly battered face, he was lucky.

Charles held out his hands, in an age-old gesture of welcome and benison. 'Come and sit down, my love, and I'll pour you a sherry.' He cleared another chair.

She sat down, still staring at him with scared eyes. He put a glass in her hand. He said, 'Don't look so worried, Liz. It's simply that our friend here punched me on the nose. Nothing that two English gentlemen can't put right in five minutes over a glass of brandy. Eh, Jocelyn?'

'Well, it's very nice of you to put it like that,' said Jocelyn.

Liz said, 'But – but how awful!' She looked at Jocelyn in wonder. 'I – just can't imagine you doing such a thing, Mr Pentecost.'

'Exactly what I've been telling him,' said Charles. 'Too easy-going by half. Still, we are what we are.'

'Anyway, I think it jolly well serves you right, Daddy,' Liz said. She turned to Jocelyn. 'I know that if *I* were a man, and married to Mrs Pentecost, and another man kissed her, I – I should kill him.'

'You see, Jocelyn?' said Charles. "What did I tell you? Another drink?'

'No, thanks. I'm driving. Or rather–? Liz, can I borrow your bicycle?'

'Of course, Mr Pentecost. I'll get it for you.'

They saw him off. 'Afraid you'll hit your knees on your chin, old man,' said Charles. 'But it's only six miles, and pretty flat.'

They watched him depart. Then they went back to the studio. 'Now, let me look at that face,' said Liz. She tut-tutted. 'Oh, Daddy, *why* did you have to spoil everything?'

'Me?' he said. 'I've not spoilt anything. Oh, old Jocelyn forgot himself for a second, but we've soon put that right. Men look at these things very differently from *your* neurotic sex, Liz.'

'But Mrs Pentecost? I shall feel terribly embarrassed. And–' she wanted to say: 'And what must Gaylord think?' But she could not. Gaylord was too private a matter to discuss with anyone. She held his name in her heart, bound with silken threads, not to be spoken to others, to be murmured only to her pillow, to be cast on the black and secret waters of the midnight river.

Charles said, 'One bit of news to cheer you up. The Erl King's wife descended on the Pentecosts' tonight and snatched away her daughter. They'll be back in Germany tomorrow.'

'Really?' Oh, this was wonderful news. With Christine out of the way Gaylord might once again notice Liz. Provided, of course, her father hadn't ruined everything with the Pentecosts forever. She would have liked to ask more. But Charles was now lost in his own thoughts. He slumped in his chair, gnawing his knuckles, his eyes blank and far away. Liz knew it was no good speaking to him when he was like this. He just wouldn't hear. The only thing was to wait for him to surface.

And suddenly he gave her a rather startled look and said, 'Promise me something, Liz.'

'Of course, Daddy.'

'If ever you have a son, don't let the poor little devil develop a Puritan conscience. But if he *does*, stop him being an artist. Stick him in a bank for God's sake.'

CHAPTER 11

So. Gaylord kissed a girl for the first time. And his world caught fire.

Charles kissed May. May slapped Charles. They had a restrained altercation. They then went back to behaving as though nothing whatever had happened; for, being English, they believed that if you pretended hard enough that nothing had happened, you would find that nothing *had* happened, and that the world would continue turning as before.

But something *had* happened. May, at forty, with the good years behind her, and before her what suddenly appeared at best a comfortable, uneventful life insulated by her family and her class – May had to admit that something *had* happened. That though her immediate reaction had been to hit him as hard as she could, other reactions missed being first only by the tiniest of split seconds: to throw her arms round him and kiss him on the lips; to burst into tears; to murmur endearments; to comfort him in his loneliness; to run to her husband and fling herself, weeping, into his arms.

But the slap on the cheek got in first, and

established the pattern: altercation, civilized behaviour, and finally a quiet, understanding word with Jocelyn about it.

The only thing was, she *hadn't* had a word with Jocelyn. To her surprise, she'd kept putting it off. Until with appalling suddenness she knew she had put it off too long, and her ordered world was out of hand and out of her control.

Nor had she yet had time to sort out her feelings of this afternoon: the heat, the drowsy peace, the presence of an attractive man whose love for her was as immanent as the summer warmth; the sudden shock of horror of the falling bird – all this had left her horribly disturbed and on edge, a very different person from the May Pentecost, wife and mother, whom she knew and secretly rather admired.

In this crisis she could have done without Frau Haldt. Nevertheless the courtesies must be observed though the heavens fall. 'Now Frau Haldt. Some coffee?'

'Thank you, no, Mrs Pentecost. My taxi is waiting, and I have rooms reserved at *The Swan Hotel* in Ingerby. Tomorrow we leave for Germany. Christine, pack your things and take them out to the taxi. Then we will depart.'

Christine gave her mother a filthy look and left the room.

Frau Haldt sat very straight, very composed, hands in lap. She was wearing a suit of simple but masterly cut. Her lips were rounded but firm, her eyes smiled into the middle distance, apparently quite uninterested in the furnishings, the pictures, or the human figures in this foreign room.

May, still keeping the worst of the bloodstains covered, said, 'Mrs Haldt?'

Frau Haldt turned slowly, raised a well-tended eyebrow, and said, 'Yes, Mrs Pentecost?'

'Mrs Haldt. It was very wrong of my son to tell Christine that I wanted an au pair girl, and I apologize for him. I also apologize for the fact that I assumed your daughter had come here with your full permission. I gather I was wrong in this assumption.'

Frau Haldt inclined her head as an acknowledgement of the apologies. She said, 'Until I received this communication I had no idea of my daughter's whereabouts.' And to Amanda's horror she took the letter from her handbag and gave it to May.

May read it. Amanda searched her mother's face, and found naught for her comfort. May said, 'I have already apologized for my son. It seems I must now apologize for my daughter.'

'That is not necessary,' Frau Haldt said quickly. 'It is thanks to her that I have found Christine.' She gave Amanda a friendly smile.

'I still apologize,' said May, giving her

179

daughter a look that Amanda classified, correctly, as absolutely foul.

Christine returned, spoke to her mother curtly in German. Frau Haldt rose, put a hand on May's arm. 'Mrs Pentecost, all these apologies are unnecessary. No harm has been done. I have had an interesting visit. And – Mrs Pentecost?'

'Yes?'

'Do not scold your young daughter too severely. She is charming. And I am sure that she thought she was acting for the best.'

'For her *own* best,' corrected May. 'I know Amanda.' She led the way out of the room. Frau Haldt glided after her. A furious Christine brought up the rear. Amanda, left alone, decided there was a great deal to be said for going to bed before Mummy returned. There was no escape from Mummy, of course. Mummy was like the Wrath of God. But if she pretended to be asleep, she just *might* get away with it; till the morning, anyway.

A taxi was waiting. The man held the door open. Christine, in an unsteady voice, said, 'Mrs Pentecost, you will understand how deeply humiliated I am by my mother's action. But – thank you for all your patience with a very unsatisfactory au pair girl.'

May kissed her impulsively. 'Goodbye, my dear. And I *do* wish you well.'

She could feel the tenseness in the girl's body. Christine kissed her, and got into the taxi. Frau Haldt held out her hand. 'Goodbye, Mrs Pentecost. I hope you will soon settle your marital difficulties.'

May was silent. The taxi moved away. May watched it, saw the red tail lights double in brightness as the driver braked to turn out of the drive. Then the taxi disappeared; and with it, thought May, an X factor she was very relieved to have out of her house; a charming, good natured, highly intelligent girl against whom she could say absolutely nothing; save that she was young, and beautiful.

Even the sound of the taxi was lost now in the still night. May turned on her heel. 'Settle my marital difficulties, indeed!' 'The higher age brackets!' 'It flatters a little, but not too much!' She found herself beginning to fume again. 'Patronizing female!'

Amanda had just got time to get into bed, close her eyes, slightly open her lips, and begin a deep, regular breathing before her mother came into the room.

To May, in her overwrought state, the sight of sleeping innocence – the near transparency of the skin, the delicate shading beneath the eyes, the tender half smile about the moist lips – was almost too much, even though she knew perfectly well that Amanda was no more asleep than she was. She would have liked to creep away, and sort out her emotions quietly, before Jocelyn came back. But she never allowed her offspring to get away with anything. 'Where is everybody?' she said.

Amanda began to give a very creditable imitation of a child rudely awakened from a deep sleep. But one look at her mother's face and she realized she was wasting her time. She sighed. 'Grandpa's in bed, Daddy went with Mr Bunting, you made him, and Gaylord went for a walk. He asked Christine but she wouldn't go, just as well or she wouldn't have been here for her mother to cart her off so satisfactorily.'

Since May had not noticed Gaylord's departure, another uneasy thought was now added to those already wriggling about in her mind. Uneasy thoughts, in fact, were multiplying at the moment like amoebas. 'You mean,' she said, 'Gaylord doesn't know about Christine leaving?'

'Not a sausage,' said Amanda with satisfaction.

So before this day was out May was going to have to deal with a husband who had suddenly changed his tweeds and Parker 61 for the skins and club of the caveman; with a son to whom she had to break news that, unless she was very much mistaken, would shatter him; with the tangled skein of her

182

own feelings; and with a ten-year-old daughter who had broken the English moral code by telling tales. Well, Amanda would have to wait. May kissed her absently. 'You can really go to sleep now,' she said. 'I'll deal with you in the morning.' She went downstairs, and made herself some Horlicks. She was just taking it through into the living room when the back door opened. She turned round. It was Gaylord, looking a little fey.

He had set off for his walk across the paddock, through the orchard, to the path that followed the river.

The old pear tree, hallowed by his having sat beneath it with Christine, wore a spangled headdress of stars.

The night was dark, and a pair of headlights was coming along the lonely river road. Late for visitors. But he wasn't interested. Christine had kissed him! She had said she would stay, if his mother would let her. Well, Mum was a good sort. If he really talked to her, explained that he and Christine simply couldn't live without each other...

She'd kissed him! Suddenly he wanted to run, to swim, to dive deep into the waters of the star-strewn river to surge forward with strength of arm and chest and thigh. He wanted to shout, exalt, yell at the arrogant stars. They might be vast, distant, immortal, yet what did they know of a woman's love?

He might be earthbound, scarcely less tran-sient than a flower. But a girl had looked on him with love. He was greater than they.

He began to run, urgently. But in the darkness he could not run with the abandon he needed. Then he remembered his beloved boat.

He groped his way along the landing stage, untied the rope with hurrying fingers, pushed off. He began to row up-stream, clumsily, urgently, the oars clattering in the rowlocks, slapping and splashing the little waves. 'In, out,' he yelled joyously. 'In, out, in out, in out, in out.' But after a time the hard exercise quietened both mind and body. He was sud-denly ashamed of his behaviour. He shipped his oars, lay back in the boat. The night was warm. The river lapped gently. From the bank he heard the contented cropping of a horse. The stars were all about him, bright in the zenith, misty at the horizon, dancing lightly below him in the black water. He was at the centre of a Fabergé Easter egg encrusted with jewels. Cradled in the soft air of the summer night, blanketed in half-senti-mental longing for the beloved, languorously in love with love – Gaylord Pentecost was at peace. It was almost an initiation. He, boy/man, was becoming part, an understand-ing part, of the life that surrounded him. His first gropings towards understanding, in the Bavarian forests, were being confirmed. Joy, sorrow, care, love, responsibility; river, trees, rocks, the kindly earth; night and day, seedtime and harvest, a mystery of stars, with all these was he now robed. He, Gaylord Pentecost, was falling into step with that unending throng that trudges forever down an unknown road: man, poised between atoms and galaxies, between heaven and hell, between agony and ecstasy – lost, blundering, inextinguishable man!

And woman! That perhaps was the key that opened the door to him. Woman, the motive force and the goal, the tempest and the haven, eternal mother and eternal prey; Alpha and Omega and Alpha, full circle, the beginning and the end and the beginning. Woman.

'Horlicks?' said May. It was not the greeting a Shakespearean mother would have given to a son she was about to stab to the heart. But it was practical. She went and found another beaker, began her preparations. Gaylord wandered round after her. 'Christine's gone to bed?' he asked in a voice whose casualness would have deceived no one, least of all his mother.

'Er, no,' said May, concentrating on mixing milk and powder.

'Where is she?'

May poured on the hot milk, stirred. 'Bring it into the living room,' she said.

They went into the living room single file,

carrying their beakers, walking carefully and with concentration, like children in a nativity play bearing gifts. She sat down. He perched on the edge of a Chippendale table. 'Your father's taking his time,' she said.

He sipped, watching her with troubled eyes. 'Where is she?' he asked again.

She said, 'Darling, Mr Chippendale didn't make that table for the twentieth century schoolboys to sit on.' She patted the arm of the chair. 'Come and sit here.'

Something *was* wrong. Her voice was tight. He went and sat on her chair arm. She took his hand, squeezed it. 'She's gone back to Germany, Gaylord.'

The silence in the room was frightening. She looked up into his face; and saw, for the first time in her child, the face of a man. 'Her mother came and took her away.'

'But–? She was here. An hour ago. She couldn't–'

'They've gone to *The Swan* at Ingerby for the night. They're flying tomorrow.'

'But–'

'Were you in love with her?'

He flushed violently. 'Good Lord, no. What an idea!' He gave the impression he scarcely understood what his mother was talking about. Then, after a decent interval, he asked, 'Did she – say anything?'

'No.'

He was silent. Then he said, 'I think I'll go

to bed, now, Mother.' He bent down, kissed her forehead. 'Good night.'

She wound an arm around his neck, holding him down. 'It – wouldn't have worked, you know, darling,' she said.

'Good night,' he said again.

She said, 'I *can* remember the pains of first love. Even at my age.' She smiled tentatively, but he was not amused. 'So if you would like to talk–? It does help, you know.'

'Thanks, Mum,' he said. He managed a smile. 'Good night.'

It was no good. She let him go. Sadly. She and Gaylord had always been able to talk. And now? Surely the Erl King's Daughter hadn't come between them? No. It wasn't the Erl King's Daughter. It was manhood, adulthood, love. She and Gaylord could no longer talk, because *her* Gaylord was suddenly dead, scorched by that fire of adult involvement in which childhood and innocence must perish. In his place, Phoenix-like, stood a grave, tormented young man who knew he must fight his battles alone.

She smiled up at him as he turned in the doorway. He smiled back. 'Good night, my darling,' she said.

He went. She wanted to cry. She had always so loved the orderliness of her world. On the rare occasions when she allowed herself a little self-congratulation, she had to admit that not every woman could achieve *her* smooth running of a house that contained her formidable old father-in-law, a husband she shared with a crowd of fictional characters, an adolescent son, and a daughter who was rather like having a poltergeist about the place. Not many women, she liked to think, could do the cooking and the cleaning and the typing and the proof reading and the riot-act-reading and the loving and the comforting and correcting – *and* remain a passably elegant and soignée English woman – *and* be loved by those about her.

And neither could she, she had suddenly discovered. For less than a week a thoroughly good-natured German girl had sojourned in her ordered house. And now – her life, if not her house, was a shambles. She could no longer talk to her son, who was desolate. She was waiting here to have an absolutely unprecedented row with her husband, provided, of course, he really had not taken leave of his senses. Both she and Jocelyn had physically assaulted their old friend Charles Bunting, which was unpardonable even though he had asked for it. She had been elegantly snubbed by a German woman.

But the greatest chaos was not in her house or her personal relationships. It was in her mind, where Charles Bunting and Christine Haldt, acting independently, had created havoc.

She couldn't stop thinking about Charles.

The hard, firm grip of his hands when he seized her shoulders. The roughness of the moustache that almost encircled his mouth. The mixture of contempt and near-worship with which he treated her. Suddenly it occurred to her that she was seeing him as one of those wolfish villains in Jacobean tragedy, and she was able to laugh at herself. Old Charles, with his Rolls Royce and his Savile Row tweeds – by John Webster out of the Slade School of Art!

She did not laugh long. That hungry, almost brutal kiss had shaken her. But why? She deeply loved her normally gentle husband. And *she* wasn't a woman who needed to be dominated. In fact, she always feared she might be a rather bossy female. So why was she disturbed? Why was she suddenly questioning her whole civilized world, the placidity of her marriage, her way of life, her simply splendid middle class values?

And if the German girl and Charles Bunting between them had made her question her civilized world, why had she been so angry and appalled when Jocelyn suddenly broke out of that world? She couldn't have it both ways. She finished her Horlicks, gave a sharp expiration of breath. 'I'm behaving like a green girl,' she told herself firmly. And then remembered, with a sudden, quiet happiness that calmed her jangling thoughts and restored a little her self-regard, those words that Charles had quoted: *'Ronsard me célébrait du temps que j'étais belle.'*

And she had slapped the face of her Ronsard.

CHAPTER 12

Jocelyn Pentecost hadn't ridden a bicycle for years.

He'd hoped he'd find it exhilarating. He didn't. It is a law of nature that, however still the weather, the cyclist will always have a headwind. And the thought of what May was going to say was anything but exhilarating. He'd never seen her look so furious as when he biffed old Charles.

So that when at last he did come face to face with his wife he was at a considerable disadvantage: breathless, dishevelled, hot, and blinking in the sudden light. 'Hello, darling,' he said, looking, sounding, and feeling sheepish.

She regarded him coolly. 'Oh, good,' she said, speaking to herself.

'Why "good"?' It was better than 'bad', but he didn't somehow think there was much joy in it for himself.

'No bruises. I thought it might have been fisticuffs again.'

'No.' He did his best to sound casual. 'It was all quite friendly. We had a drink together. Then I came home.'

'Well, bully for you! A man forces his attentions on your wife, and before the week's out you and he are drinking together, dear old pals.'

As usual, she'd got him on the wrong foot. And Jocelyn's brain, though excellent in many ways, hadn't a high degree of manoeuvrability. Changing tack always took time. And he couldn't help feeling that Charles' cognac was clouding the issue for him. He said, 'Well, at least I biffed him when I found out about it.'

'You certainly did. I couldn't believe my eyes. You, brawling like a D.H. Lawrence miner!'

'I didn't brawl,' he said sulkily.

'Of course you brawled.'

They glared at each other. He was still prowling uneasily about the room. He said, 'It was atavism. I was telling old Charles how I once gnawed your elbow.'

She sprang to her feet, furious. 'Well, that's the last straw. Not only drinking with the man who assaulted me; but telling him the more intimate details of our married life. What a time you two must have had.'

'It wasn't like that. You remember, you turned over and accidentally stuck your elbow in my mouth and I bit you.'

'Of course I remember. I still carry the scars.'

They confronted each other, both angry, both hating the battle, yet both, like soldiers who long for the battle to stop, knowing that to stop it was quite outside their power.

So they stood. And now he remembered – a source of resentment he had almost forgotten. And resentment, at the moment, was as precious as powder and shot. He said, 'I think I deserved better than to hear it from Amanda and my father.'

She said, 'You don't *really* think–' Her anger choked her so much that she had to pause for breath – 'you don't really think I was trying to keep it from you? Oh, you *fool*, Jocelyn.'

'Well, you certainly took your time.'

'What did you expect me to do? Come running upstairs to tell you Charles had kissed me?'

'No, but – well, we always – I thought you'd have come and talked it over in a civilized manner.'

'You're a fine one to talk about civilized manners.'

He ignored this. 'It – just wasn't like you, May, to keep it to yourself.' Now his voice was reproachful, rather than angry.

Why *had* she kept it to herself? Frankly, she didn't know. But she did know it had put her at a serious tactical disadvantage. Suddenly she moved towards him. He looked startled. But she wound her arms around his neck and nuzzled her cheek against his, and said, 'Oh, Jocelyn, I'm so *miserable*.'

No one ever appealed in vain to Jocelyn's better nature. Appealed to, Jocelyn's better nature behaved like a terrier who hears the word 'walkies'. It was at the front door, wagging its tail. 'Come and sit down,' he said gently. They went and sat side by side on the settee. He crossed to the sideboard, came back with a dry Martini for her. 'What's the trouble?' he said. He was worried. It wasn't like May to ask for help.

She sipped her Martini, gave him a wan but grateful smile. 'Lots of things,' she said.

He waited.

She said, 'That German woman. She made me feel small, and cheap.'

He squeezed her hand. 'What happened?'

'She took Christine off. As from a house of ill fame. I handled it badly, Jocelyn. I handled Christine's arrival badly. I didn't button it up.' She drained her Martini. 'I'm getting old, Jocelyn. *You* know how I *always* used to have things buttoned up.'

He fetched her another Martini. 'And Gaylord,' she said, 'I handled him badly, too. We – couldn't talk. I couldn't help him. He wouldn't let me.' She looked at her husband piteously.

He was silent. She said, 'I always knew

exactly what to say to Gaylord. I don't any more.'

'It's not your fault,' he said. 'They grow up. At a certain age they fence themselves in. They don't want your help.' He sat, looking at her with the thoughtful, faraway look she knew so well. 'They resent us because they have been dependant on us. Now they want to slough us off until, in thirty years or so, *we* shall be helpless and dependent on them. Then, kindly, conscientiously, competently, they will take their revenge.'

She looked at him in surprise. 'Gaylord's not like that,' she said. Her voice was flat.

'It isn't Gaylord,' he said. 'Or us. It's the generations.'

'You're talking nonsense,' she said, without conviction.

'*I* thought I was. It's Charles' cognac. Yet all the time I was talking I kept thinking: I could be right.'

She looked at him almost fearfully. Then she said, 'I'm miserable for another reason, Jocelyn.'

'What's that?'

She said slowly, 'In my heart, I wanted Charles to go on kissing me.'

'Have another Martini?'

'Yes, please.'

He came back with a full glass, sat down, took her free hand in both of his. 'You mean you're in love with him?'

'No. 'Course not. It's just that – well, at my age it's flattering to have someone like Charles in love with you. And something is telling you to make the most of it, because it will never happen again, never, never, never. Something is telling you that you will look back from the empty years and curse your own – pusillanimity.'

'Or be thankful for your own honour,' he said quietly.

They looked at each other gravely. She said, 'A strange thing happened this afternoon. Something I found curiously upsetting. Charles and I were sitting under the elms, talking.' He looked at her with raised eyebrows, but she went on. 'There was a clatter in one of the high elms, and a bird fell almost at our feet. It lifted its wings and its head, like those old pictures of the rising phoenix. Then it – just died. It was curiously upsetting,' she repeated.

'Yes. I can imagine.'

'It seemed like an omen. But of what?'

He looked at her anxiously. Down to earth May had never been one for omens. But – a loyal, honourable woman talking alone with a man who attracted her more than she felt she ought to be attracted? A beautiful woman who was beginning to realize, for the first time, that beauty was inevitably passing? Might not such a one grow fearful of omens? 'Of what?' he echoed her.

'Of death? A bird, flying in the sunlight, or resting in the high green branches. And then, five minutes later, a shallow, dusty grave. Should we not fly in the sunlight while we may, Jocelyn?'

He shook his head. 'We're not birds, May. We walk the earth. We can do no other.'

She laid her head on his shoulder. 'Oh, Jocelyn. I do love you. But the bird. It was so beautiful, sleek, all greys and blues. And perfect. And the earth went on him.'

'Oh, May,' he said. 'Poor May. What *is* the matter with you?'

Gaylord began to panic. He had never suffered with insomnia before. But tonight he heard the clock strike eleven, then twelve, and now it must be getting on for one. He peered at the friendly dial of his luminous watch. Twelve twenty. What time did it get light? Another four, five hours. A chap couldn't exist all that time. Yet sleep was far away, and he was wretched.

Liz Bunting was also awake. What did it matter that Miss Haldt had gone back to Germany? A fine woman like Mrs Pentecost would never let her son go on meeting the daughter of a man who – she could not bring herself to formulate the thought. But it was too shaming. She hoped she would never meet any of the Pentecosts again. She wouldn't be able to look them in the face.

Charles Bunting went downstairs and made himself a cup of tea. Nose, eyes, lips, teeth and gums all felt as though they had been through a combine harvester. There was a taste of blood in his throat. It wouldn't surprise him if something wasn't badly damaged. It was so easy to neglect a thing like this, and then, before you knew where you were, the consultant chap was pursing his lips and saying, 'Had you come to me a year ago, my dear fellow, I could have saved you.'

He sat at the kitchen table, sipping his tea. It scalded his bruised lips damnably. The kitchen had the bleak, impersonal look all kitchens have at one in the morning. The night was warm but he shivered. A fever? He took his temperature. 98.4 degrees. He'd had a feeling for some time that this damned thermometer had stuck.

God he was lonely. A man like him needed a woman about the house, and not just for the obvious reasons. Sensitive, and an artist, he needed the softness and comfort and understanding that only a woman was capable of. Of course, he wouldn't disturb young Liz for anything. But he couldn't help feeling slightly aggrieved that she hadn't heard him come downstairs. Pouring himself another cup of tea, he put the teapot back on the stand with something of a clatter. Quite inadvertently, of course. He did hope it hadn't wakened Liz. It hadn't.

He thought of Rachel his wife who, noblewoman though she undoubtedly was, had never treated his various ailments with quite the seriousness they deserved. He thought of May Pentecost, in his view a perfect wife and mother. Well, he'd soon found what happened when you trespassed, however tentatively, on a happy marriage. Dear May! She'd got a kick like a mule. He did hope he hadn't spoilt his friendship with the Pentecosts. It would be such a pity. Besides, he *must* complete that portrait.

He thought of Frau Haldt, who would have made such a splendid portrait, and who had passed straight out of his life almost before she entered it. Now there was a woman: tender, feminine, lovely. He remembered the healing touch of her fingers on his unhappy nose. A woman who would care for a man in misfortune, who would walk tall beside him in success. He thought of a whole world of such creatures, born for one purpose only: to tend and comfort and succour their sons, and other woman's sons. So he sat, in his one-a-clock-in-the-morning kitchen, lonely and comfortless.

CHAPTER 13

There were quite a few surprises the following morning.

Gaylord was surprised to find that, despite his agony of mind, physically he felt quite robust. He had not expected to be able to drag himself from his bed. Yet here he was, cycling through the early morning to Ingerby; and but for his agony of mind he would have been quite enjoying it.

Christine Haldt was *very* surprised, taken aback even, when Roger Miles walked into her hotel bedroom as the clock struck eight. He was wearing a white linen jacket and carrying a tray of tea.

Roger Miles was surprised, taken aback even, when the tumble of hair on the pillow of No. 17 parted to show him the astonished but beautiful features of Christine Haldt.

Christine pulled the bedclothes tightly up to her throat and demanded, 'Captain Miles, what are you doing in my bedroom?'

'Helping out with the morning calls. It's my father's hotel,' explained Roger. 'But – why aren't you at the Pentecosts'?' His surprise had quickly given way to delight.

Talk about being handed something on a plate! He put the tray on the bedside table, sat down on the side of the bed, and leaned over and picked up the teapot. 'Now. Let me pour you a cup.'

'Captain Miles, it is not seemly. Besides, I do not order tea, there is some mistake. Please go.'

'I can't. You haven't answered my question.'

A terrible voice from the doorway said, 'So, this again is the English permissiveness, then. The hotel bellhop sits himself on the bed and pours the tea for the lady visitors.'

Roger rose calmly to his feet. 'I am not the bellhop, madam. I am the son of the proprietor,' he said pleasantly.

'And in England it is impolite to speak of bellhops, *Mutti*,' said Christine. 'The idiom is American, and vulgar.'

'At this moment,' said Frau Haldt, 'I am not interested in idiom.'

Christine said, '*Mutti*, this is the Captain Miles. He is a friend of Gaylord Pentecost.'

'And also a cousin of the Queen, I suppose,' said Frau Haldt nastily.

'Only distant, I'm afraid,' said Roger.

Christine said, 'And this is my mother, who is taking me back to Germany.'

Roger bowed. 'How do you do?' Then he looked appalled. 'But madam, you cannot be so cruel as to take your daughter away from us?'

'How do you do? I most certainly can. And now, if you will kindly leave my daughter's bedroom, we have to make our final plans for the journey.'

Gaylord did what any lover would have done in the circumstances. He twisted the knife in his heart by going to watch the final departure of the beloved.

During the night he had examined a dozen possibilities, from pleading with Frau Haldt to elopement. None of them had offered much in the way of hope. So now he just leaned on his bicycle in the Market Square and watched *The Swan*.

Nor had he waited five minutes before a taxi drew up outside the hotel, a porter carried out bags and skis and ski sticks, and then Christine and her mother appeared. Christine got into the car. Her mother stayed and tipped the porter. Well, at least he had a chance to speak to Christine. If only to say, 'Write to me!' There might even be time for a fleeting kiss – a kiss, he thought with bitter pain that would have to last him for a lifetime.

He stepped eagerly off the kerb – and an open Rolls Royce, its horn uttering dignified protest, reared up on its haunches a foot away from him. 'What the devil do you think you're playing at, young Gaylord?' demanded Charles Bunting.

'Sorry, Mr Bunting. I didn't hear you.'

'You're not supposed to hear me in this car, dammit. But you've got eyes, haven't you?'

'Yes, Mr Bunting.' The street was crowded with buses and lorries. He couldn't get a glimpse of the taxi.

'Ah, well. Lucky I'm a good driver. But what are you doing in this God-forsaken town at this God-forsaken hour?'

The traffic cleared for a moment. Gaylord saw to his relief that the taxi was still there, and Frau Haldt was still talking to the porter. 'Excuse me, Mr Bunting,' he said courteously but urgently. But then he saw something else: Roger Miles, bending down with his head through the taxi window. Talking to Christine. Why, he could easily be kissing Christine! And, even as Gaylord watched, Frau Haldt got into the car, the porter shut the door and saluted, Roger withdrew his head and smiled and waved, and smiled and waved, and the taxi pulled into the traffic and was gone.

'Excuse you what for?' said Charles.

'Oh, nothing, Mr Bunting,' said Gaylord.

Charles gave him a funny look. It had never occurred to him before, but he didn't think Gaylord seemed one of the brightest. He hoped Liz knew what she was doing. He said, 'I've come in early to see how they've hung my pictures for the exhibition. Sure to have got them all wrong. Between ourselves, the only ones they're interested in are the nudes.'

'Really?' The taxi would be in the suburbs now. Soon it would be on the dual carriageway leading to the Airport. Christine was being whisked out of his life at 30, 40, 60, 600 miles an hour. And all he could do was stand there talking.

'They pick 'em out, you know, hang 'em in prominent positions, and just stick the rest round them.'

'Really?'

'Really.' He gave Gaylord another questioning look. It occurred to him that Gaylord's behaviour was very much like Liz's this morning. She, too, had given the impression she just wasn't listening to a word. He said, 'Look. Liz was a bit down in the mouth this morning. Why don't you go and cheer her up? Play tennis or something?' He groped in his pocket. 'Here. Here's a fiver. Take her out of herself.'

'Mr Bunting, I couldn't possibly.'

'Dear boy, don't be daft. A lot of things in this life are difficult. But accepting a fiver isn't one of them.' He stuffed it into Gaylord's breast pocket. 'Now I have to swing across two streams of traffic into that damned bolt hole *The Swan* calls its carriage entrance. Wish me luck.'

'Good luck, Mr Bunting.'

'Thanks.' He touched the indicator switch, swung away from the curb at ninety degrees, and took a direct course to *The Swan*. The effect on the Ingerby morning rush-hour traffic was briefly chaotic. But the English are very tolerant of eccentric behaviour on the part of Rolls Royces. They feel, rightly, that it is part of the English heritage.

After her father had left for Ingerby, Liz Bunting did a quick review of her life; and confirmed one of the things she had decided last night: that she could never, in any circumstances, meet one of the Pentecosts again. Especially not Gaylord. She didn't know much about psychology. But she imagined that the son's feelings for the daughter of the man who had made unwelcome advances to his mother must inevitably have been the subject of a play by Sophocles and a complex by Freud, and could consist only of contempt, hatred and bitterness.

So that when, looking out of the window, she saw Gaylord ambling from side to side of the drive on his bicycle, she tiptoed quietly upstairs and stood, scarcely breathing, but heart pounding, on the landing.

The front door bell rang. It rang again. Then: 'Liz, where are you, Liz?'

She was absolutely still. He called again. Then she heard him open the door and call again. Then the door shut.

Was he in the house? Or had he gone? She crept across to a window, looked out.

He was pushing his bicycle back down the drive, occasionally glancing in a puzzled way at the house.

A few more seconds and he would be at the gate, jumping on his bicycle and away. She yearned for him. She *couldn't* let him go. Blow Sophocles, blow Freud. 'Gaylord,' she shouted. 'Gaylord! Wait!'

He heard her, checked. She tore downstairs, out at the front door, down the drive, arms outstretched, still calling his name. She ran up to him.

But not, alas, into his arms. 'Hello,' he said. 'I thought you were out.'

'Sorry,' she gasped. 'I was upstairs. Making the beds,' she lied.

They would be at the Airport by now, in the Departure Lounge. She would be sitting there, calm, beautiful, thinking of – whom? Why, Roger Miles, of course, he told himself sadly. Who would ever think of Gaylord Pentecost when they could think about Roger Miles?

He said, 'Your father gave me this. To take you out. Where would you like to go?'

The one question in her mind had been: why has he come? Is he turning back to me now Christine has gone? She hadn't really thought so. He hadn't the air of one who has suddenly said to himself, 'Young Liz is the girl for me.' Still, she could always hope.

And now hope was quenched. Her father,

well meaning no doubt, had give him a fiver to keep her amused! *That* was why he was here.

Well, Liz wasn't one to be hoity-toity. She said, 'You don't *have* to take me out, Gaylord. It's only if *you* want to.'

He wondered what time the plane took off. They might be calling the flight now. He said, '*I* don't mind. We'd better do *something*. It's very generous of your father.'

She'd heard more enthusiastic acceptances. She said, 'It doesn't matter, Gaylord. Really.'

Or he supposed the aeroplane could have crashed now. *Within seconds of take off*, they often said. He spent a little time beside her hospital bed, willing her back to life. Then he said, 'I can't think of *anything* that would cost five pounds.'

She said, boldly, 'Anything would be nice with you, Gaylord.'

He accepted this. 'But five *pounds*,' he said.

'*I* know,' she said, suddenly almost gay. 'Let's go out for lunch.'

'Right ho,' he said, without enthusiasm. 'Get your bike.'

A dreadful thought struck her. 'Gaylord, I can't.'

'Why not?'

'I lent it – someone.' Another moment, and the dreadful affair of their parents would have been rearing up between them. But she had avoided it. 'I know. We'll have a taxi. And anyway, I didn't mean cycle. I meant I'd dress up and – and do my face–'

It all sounded potty to Gaylord. But Liz seemed to like the idea, and he supposed that if they had a taxi and went somewhere sufficiently expensive there wouldn't be so much change out of a fiver. And anyway, what did it matter what he did with his *life* from now on, let alone a single day?

But to Liz it sounded very heaven. 'Now you be deciding where to go while I change. Then we'll ring up for a taxi.' She ran upstairs. She tied her hair into her favourite ponytail, put on lipstick and eye shadow. She glanced out of the window. A lovely, sleepy, balmy summer's day. It would be hot by lunchtime. She put on a cool, cotton frock patterned with flowers. She found some white sandals and a white handbag. Looking at herself in the mirror she was quite impressed. It was a change from denims. Oh, she hadn't the German girl's chic, of course. But she really did think that, if you wanted an *English* rose, she wasn't too bad.

And I bet he won't even look at me, she thought.

Nor did he, when she first came into the room. He simply rose, looked out of the window, and said, 'It's going to be hot.' Then suddenly she saw him spot her frock and look impressed. She waited for his comment, lips parted, a half smile on her face. 'It's the same pattern as our chair covers,' he said.

'*Is* it, Gaylord?' she said, trying to sound as impressed as he. 'Now, have you thought where you'd like to go for lunch?'

'No. There doesn't seem to be anywhere.'

'You would – *like* to go?' she said anxiously.

''Course.' Perhaps she was crossing the English coast now. Looking down on a silver painted pier, a line of foam, a sparkling sea. Perhaps she had left England behind, never to return. He wanted to howl like a dog.

Liz said, 'There's a place Daddy likes. It's on the river near Shepherd's Warning, and you can eat out of doors when it's nice. It'd be super on a day like this.'

'Is it expensive?'

'I should think so.'

'Right,' he said listlessly.

She said, 'Oh, Gaylord, I don't think you want to go a bit.'

At last the disappointment in her voice and face got through to him. He pulled himself together, grinned. 'Of course I do. I'll telephone for a taxi. Now what's this place called?'

The Linden Tree was sufficiently expensive, even for Gaylord. On a terrace overhanging the river, shaded by limes and willows, stood tables sparkling with glass and silver. Gaylord and Liz, wandering vaguely towards it over a cropped lawn, were approached by a head waiter in tails who, so far neutral and watchful, was prepared to adopt in a moment the manner of a gentleman farmer coping with trespassers, or of a Grand Vizier welcoming his Sultan, depending on his immediate assessment of these teenagers' social standing, behaviour, and possibly cash flow.

Gaylord and Liz found this brisk approach unnerving. Nevertheless, they fought off the desire to bolt, and stood their ground.

'Sir, madam?' said the man. 'You are looking for–?'

'We wondered whether you could give us lunch?' said Liz winsomely.

'Our pleasure, madam.' The man looked relieved. He'd been afraid it was going to be a couple of Cokes. 'This way, madam, sir.'

He led them to the terrace, and to a table for two. Gaylord said to Liz, 'Coke? Or–?' He decided to take the head waiter into his confidence. 'Ought we to have sherry?'

The head waiter actually smiled. 'A dry sherry would be – appropriate.'

'Then we'll have two dry sherries,' said Gaylord.

They raised their glasses. 'Cheers,' said Gaylord. 'Cheers,' said Liz. They sipped. It was very dry, very thin, very horrible, they both thought. Why anyone drank this when they could have Coke–? Still, there was one thing about it. It did make you feel terribly grown up and sophisticated. And the sun beamed and the river chortled and the waterfowl chuckled and the head waiter, who was largely French, was now so enchanted by these two delightful children that his aura was as warm as the sun's. Liz said, 'Oh Gaylord, isn't it all heavenly!' (But it wasn't all heavenly. Liz was one of those nice but unfortunate people who can be happy only when those about them are happy. And she knew that Gaylord, despite his obvious efforts to enter into the spirit of the outing, was as miserable as sin.) 'I've only been to this sort of place with Daddy,' she said. 'But it's much more fun with you, Gaylord.'

'Yes,' he said. He wondered how long letters took from Germany. Weeks, probably. So it was no use looking for one just yet, even if she had any intention of writing. Yet he knew he would be watching desperately for the postman from tomorrow morning on.

The French of the vast menu bore little relation to the French they did at school. So once again they took the fatherly waiter into their confidence and told him that what they would really like would be tomato soup, plaice and chips, and strawberry ice cream. And they got it. Gaylord was rather relieved. Some of the prices in the menu made even his sudden wealth look inadequate. But they couldn't charge much for plaice and chips and ice cream.

O God, let it go on forever, prayed Liz. The sun was warm on her cheek, the shadows of the trees danced and cavorted on the table cloth, if you looked up the leaves were green, translucent, glowing with an inner light. The river danced and sparkled. All nature was joyous. And here she and Gaylord sat, like a grown up couple, like an engaged or married couple, in the sweet and holy communion of a shared meal. How many more meals would they share, she wondered. Perhaps this would be the last. The first and the last. She wanted to cry.

Two swans sailed into view, pecking disdainfully with their painted beaks at the waterweeds. 'Oh, look. Swans,' said Liz. Oh, happy, monogamous swans, gliding together down the river of life, joined forever by mutual love and affection, and by the moral code of swans presumably, until, after many a summer, one broke a lifetime's silence by singing his swan song, and left his mate comfortless. Liz wanted to cry even more.

But the word 'Swan' had only one connotation for Gaylord: what cruel fate had taken Christine to the Ingerby *Swan*, where she had been certain to meet Roger Miles, to come again under the spell of Roger Miles' charm, to have any memories she might have of Gaylord Pentecost sponged from her mind by the *charisma* of Roger

Miles! Not that Gaylord had any disloyal thoughts about Roger, of course. It was just that two such perfect creatures as Roger and Christine would naturally be attracted one to the other. Anyone as inferior as he would hardly impinge on their consciousness.

And yet – she had kissed him, she had looked at him with eyes of love. Yes. But since then she'd met Miles again. No girl who'd met Miles again would remember Gaylord.

Liz said, 'Super plaice! Do you remember that little fish and chip shop in Wales? I don't think this is quite as nice as we had there. But it's very good.'

'We were younger then,' said Gaylord. Young and carefree, he thought, and untormented. Ah, the cheerful appetite, the untroubled sleep of youth! He sighed. He didn't suppose he'd ever have a good night sleep, or really enjoy a meal, ever again.

Liz, hearing the sigh, looked at him with troubled eyes. Poor Gaylord! Poor, poor Gaylord. His sorrow was her sorrow, must always be her sorrow. That was what love was all about. She said, 'I'm sorry Christine's gone back, Gaylord.'

'You are?' He looked surprised. It hadn't occurred to him that Liz and Christine were buddies. Then he understood. 'Oh, you were looking forward to some more tennis lessons.'

'No. I meant – for your sake, Gaylord.'

'Oh, that.' He coloured. But at seventeen (or perhaps at any age in England) emotions must always be concealed or dissembled. So he said, 'No. It didn't bother me. I'd just thought it would be nice for my mother to have some help. She's getting on a bit, you know.'

'But she's wonderful for her age,' said Liz, springing to the defence of her adored Mrs Pentecost.

'Oh, wonderful,' agreed Gaylord, rather pleased at the deft way he had changed the subject.

The waiter brought the ice cream. It nestled in silver dishes. The dishes, starred with tiny beads of moisture, rested on lace doilies, beneath which was a plate bearing a silver spoon. Liz who, in spite of her concern for Gaylord, was enjoying her food enormously, took a spoonful, looked ecstatic, and said, '*Super* ice cream.'

Gaylord regarded himself as something of a connoisseur of ice cream. He took a spoonful with the air of a maître d'hôtel trying the soup. 'Walls,' he said knowledgeably.

'Is it really?' said Liz, deeply impressed.

He nodded. 'You can always tell Walls.' He took another spoonful, nodded again. 'It's easily my favourite.'

Liz ate her last spoonful. And thought: it's

nearly over. This dappled scene, this happy sunlight; we shall walk away, and the table will be cleared, and the cloth changed for other diners, and the sun will go down behind the poplars, and it will be as though we had never been. And the two swans will glide away together, like creatures of fairy tale. And our happy day will be done.

But they lingered over their coffee, while Liz watched the afternoon shadows stealing across the lawn, and Gaylord thought: she could have landed at Munich by now; she could be on that wide sweeping road that leads to the mountains and the deep forests; the dark forests that will swallow her up forever.

The waiter brought the bill. Gaylord unfolded it in a casual, worldly manner. He read the amount as though it was a matter of no concern for a bon viveur like himself. Which was really creditable, since it was for slightly more than he had in his pocket.

They *couldn't* charge all that for plaice and chips! But they had. He was really very scared. But he maintained his English sang froid. 'You don't happen to have a ten pence, do you, Liz? It doesn't matter, only— Just a question of change.'

The few seconds while she searched in her bag were some of the worst he had known. Then she said, 'Yes. Here you are, Gaylord.'

'Oh, thanks. Sure you can spare it?'

'Of course.'

He was sweating with anxiety. He paid the waiter (service, he was thankful to see, was included). As they left the terrace, the head waiter bowed, which he did to everyone, and smiled, which he did to very few. So unusual nowadays to see a pair of young lovers with style – a style and a breathtaking innocence that wrung his Gallic withers.

They walked across the lawn. The sun was still hot, but the shadows were beginning to lengthen. Their day together was ending. Liz thought how pleasant it would be to stroll home through the quiet lanes. Perhaps, if she got too tired, Gaylord would let her take his arm. Or perhaps, if he continued so sad, she could slip her hand into his, purely by way of comfort, of course. She had a most moving picture of herself and Gaylord walking hand in hand into the setting sun. But it was only a dream. It must be a good seven miles to her father's cottage. Gaylord would think her potty if she suggested walking that far. 'Shall we ring up from the hotel for a taxi?' she said sadly. (Another half hour and she'd be at home, and Gaylord would be cycling off to The Cypresses.)

But to her surprise (and delight) he said, 'Actually, I wouldn't mind walking. But I suppose you–?'

'Gaylord, I'd *love* to walk. It's only seven miles. And it's such a lovely afternoon.'

Well, *that* was a relief. When you haven't even got enough money to ring up for a taxi, walking is a very satisfactory idea. (So, though this did not occur to Gaylord, is a girl who is willing to trudge the seven miles with you.)

So they strolled home, through the mellow, honeyed, sun-drenched September after-noon, through the lanes of meadow sweet and Queen Anne's lace, through fields starred with autumn crocus, past orchards where pears and apples and plums held all the summer's sweetness. They walked like the old friends they were, saying little, their conversation grave, and with something of the melancholy inseparable from an autumn day, their hearts heavy: his because seas and mountains and appalling distances must now separate him from his loved one; she because her loved one, though he walked by her side, was in the spirit a thousand miles away.

They walked side by side, untouching. Other girls would have used a dozen ploys to make contact: weariness, a blister on the foot, slipping on a stile, needing a hand to cross a stream. Liz, though as much woman as any of them, had an uncompromising honesty that would let her do none of these things. She *was* weary. She *had* a blister on her heel. But she trudged on, uncomp-laining, independent, gravely cheerful. Only when they reached her father's cottage did she say, 'I suppose you wouldn't want to come in? I could cook us a meal.'

'No, thanks,' he said. 'Mother will wonder where I've got to.'

'Of course,' she said. She gave him a sad, loving smile. 'Oh, Gaylord, it *has* been a lovely day. Thank you ever so much.'

'It was your father's idea,' he said. 'And he paid for it. Oh Lord,' he remembered. 'I owe you ten pence.'

'That's all right. Thanks, Gaylord. It was a day,' she said – and her voice trembled a little – 'a day I shall always remember.'

'Me, too,' he said. The day Christine went back to Germany! It would be graven on his heart.

She tried once more. 'Sure you won't stay for supper?'

'Sure, thanks. So long, Liz.' He sat astride his bicycle, legs dangling, and coaxed his bike down the drive. At the gate he turned. 'So long, Liz.'

'So long, Gaylord.' She stood watching for a long time, hoping for a glimpse of him along the road. Then she went inside. Father was not yet home. She cooked herself eggs and bacon. Then she went upstairs, and cried herself to sleep.

Having had an au pair to help her for a few days, May went back to doing all the work herself with a sense of relief and relaxation. Things were so *easy*. The only trouble was Gaylord, about whom she felt much as Gertrude felt about Hamlet in Act 1. 'Good Hamlet, cast thy nighted colour off,' was frequently on the tip of her tongue. But she never said it. Gaylord didn't look in the mood for literary allusions.

Her other worries concerned Charles.

She wanted to see him, to talk to him. Having her portrait painted had been a wonderful interlude. To sit there, enjoying his company, little said between them, while he tried to recreate what he saw as her beauty; to sit there with, in her heart, a feeling of friendship as warm and sweet as the long summer afternoons... (Yes, warm and sweet, an emotion that filled her whole being with contentment. But was friendship the right word? She could not bring herself to face this question.) But then – all this had come to a sudden end, with a bird falling mysteriously from the sky, and with an unbelievable explosion from Jocelyn. Since then, she had heard nothing. What ought she to do? Telephone him, find out which way the wind lay? That was what she wanted to do. But there was Jocelyn – a new Jocelyn, wary and prickly where Charles was concerned. For the first time in their married life, she couldn't assume that Jocelyn would go along with anything she did.

So one day, as they drank their after-lunch coffee on the lawn, she said, 'Darling, do you think you ought to give old Charles a ring sometime? We've not heard from him for ages.'

Jocelyn said, 'It's a bit awkward. That night, after a drink or two, it seemed all right. But now, not having anything, one wonders–'

For a man to whom words were his livelihood, thought May, there were times when Jocelyn verged surprisingly on the inarticulate. Still, she got the gist of it. He didn't want to. She said, 'The trouble is, the longer we put it off the more difficult it will be?'

'It's tricky,' he agreed. She waited, hoping for a more positive response. None came. She said, 'Would you rather we didn't try to repair the friendship? Just left things?'

'Good Lord, no. We've been friends for years.'

'I just wondered,' she said. 'You did rather get on your high horse, didn't you. I really was rather scared.'

That made his day. Of course, the last thing he wanted was to scare anyone, let alone his wife. Still, perhaps it wasn't such a bad thing, very occasionally, to do a bit of sabre rattling. A chap, especially an absent-minded writer chap like him, could too easily let himself be taken for granted. Didn't do any harm to let them realize he'd got his finger on the pulse, knew how many

219

beans made five, knew, in fact, exactly what was going on. He said, 'Look, May, you go and telephone old Charles. Ask him round to supper. And – if he's stuffy, just tell him not to be a fat-head.'

She looked doubtful. 'Well, if you're sure that's all right with you–?'

'Of course.'

He answered the telephone himself. She said, 'Hello, Charles. So you *haven't* emigrated.'

'Oh, hello old girl. No, still in my ain countree and paying eighty-three pence in the pound for the privilege.'

He sounded cheerful and light-hearted. But she wasn't at all sure he'd got her point. She said, 'I meant we haven't seen you for ages.'

'No. Sorry about that, May. Up to my eyes in work, as usual.'

'Why don't you and Liz drop in for supper one evening? Before Gaylord goes back to school?'

'Love to, May. But – just at the moment–'

There *was* something wrong. She'd suspected it even before she lifted the receiver. She had a cold feeling in her stomach. She said, 'Charles?'

'Yes, old girl?'

'There's – nothing the matter, is there? You're not furious with us?'

'Good Lord, no. Why should I be?'

'Well, I did rather belt you one. And old Jocelyn – but he does have these attacks of atavism, you know. He once bit my elbow.'

'So he told me. No. You're still my favourite couple, bless you. I'll be seeing you.'

'Any time, Charles. You know that.'

She put down the receiver, very unhappy. To have hurt an old friend, a man who by his solitary and prickly nature found friendship difficult! Of course, he shouldn't have kissed her. But they need not have reacted quite so angrily. And if he really *did* love her – poor man, he must have had a miserable time.

Still, he'd sounded cheerful; amused, even. Almost as though he was deliberately announcing his freedom from an irksome relationship. Oh, Charles had often been rude to her. That was Charles. But today he hadn't been rude. He'd been cheerful and friendly. Yet she felt he had snubbed her. She felt cheap.

And the portrait! He hadn't mentioned it.

Of course, it didn't matter. But now she realized for the first time how much she had been looking forward to it, how much it meant to her to be painted by Charles Bunting, Esquire, not for money but because he loved her and thought her beautiful and wished to give her beauty immortality. And how many times recently had she murmured to herself, with a warm, happy feeling, in the secrecy of her woman's soul: *'Ronsard me célébrait du temps que j'étais belle.'*

And now, no portrait. Another unfinished canvas chucked into a corner, to be torn up to light a fire in a winter's dusk!

Jocelyn said, 'Did you telephone old Charles?'

'Yes. He's quite all right. No hard feelings. But he's awfully busy at present.'

He got the message. He too felt depressed. Oh, Charles would come round. But – to Jocelyn, as to May, discord of any kind was an unhappy business.

Nor did Gaylord do anything to relieve their depression. He was touchy. He'd have been irritable if May had let him be. He was listless, and spent most of his time mooning about in his precious boat. The only times he showed a furtive interest was when the postman came. But there was never anything for him.

CHAPTER 14

It was the last day of the summer holidays.

And thank goodness for that, thought May. Gaylord was getting her down. She was sorry for him; but the old cheerful, easy relationship between mother and son was gone, perhaps forever. And she couldn't get through to him. The sooner he went back to school the better. Give him something else to think about.

The last day of Gaylord's summer holidays: a day, inevitably, of sadness and nostalgia; of looking back and wondering what on earth had happened to two months of glorious summer, of regret for days heedlessly wasted, for happy days fled forever; a day of looking forward to a term of futile effort, Goethe and Racine and Euclid, vaulting horse and parallel bars, Rugby and hockey – what did any of them matter compared with a soft cheek, a cascade of hair smooth as a chestnut, eyes that had once looked love?

The last day of Gaylord's summer holidays. Liz, waking, thought: this time tomorrow he'll be cycling off to the station. She looked out of the window: a perfect, still, September day. And when he comes back it will be Christmas. The leaves will have fallen, and the first snows, the fields will be grey and mired, summer will have changed to winter. A long, long parting. She couldn't bear it! Yet bear it she must.

She hadn't seen or heard from him since that happy day at *The Linden Tree*. It would be too awful if he just went off to school without even telephoning her. That again she couldn't bear.

Nor, of course, did she have to. If he hadn't come round to say goodbye or telephoned, by mid-morning, she would ring him up. Even a member of the Upper Fifth couldn't object to an old friend wanting to wish him a successful term.

After breakfast May said, 'Now Gaylord, are your cases ready? British Rail will be calling for them any time now.'

'I think so,' he said.

'"Thinking's" no good. I had to post your rugger boots on last term.' She suddenly exploded. 'Gaylord, pull yourself together!'

Lord, she thought. I'm beginning to become a nagger. But injecting any life into Gaylord was like trying to turn over a car with a flat battery.

The telephone rang. She answered it. 'Hello, May,' said a man's voice.

'Charles!' she cried. 'Oh, how nice to hear from you.' She was trembling in her anxiety to sound natural.

'Look, sorry it's such short notice, but would you care to come to an unveiling this evening?'

'An unveiling? Love to, Charles, You mean – all of us? The children? The entire brood?'

'Good. Seven thirty for eight, then. In the Trent Room at *The Swan*.'

'Charles, this *is* exciting. Whose–?'

'Be seeing you then. Goodbye, May.'

Gaylord had disappeared – to fasten his

cases, she hoped. She went up to her husband's study. She felt as though a great weight had lifted from her shoulders. 'Darling, Charles has asked us all to an unveiling tonight. At *The Swan*. I'm so pleased. I have a feeling all is forgiven.'

'Oh, good.' He, too, sounded immensely relieved. 'I didn't like to think of old Charles– What's he unveiling? Could it be your portrait?'

That, for May, was a very important question indeed, though she would never have formulated it herself. 'I don't think it could be,' she said. 'I only had a few sittings. I imagine there was a lot more work to be done.'

'No. It doesn't seem likely,' he said disappointingly.

'No.' But she'd jolly well go on hoping. Of course it would be terribly embarrassing among a lot of strangers to have a cloth whisked off an easel, and see oneself underneath, probably not looking at all as one felt one really looked, and everyone clapping, and looking at the portrait, then coming up and peering at one. Like that patronizing German woman, she remembered. 'A little flattering. But not much.' Terribly embarrassing.

But jolly nice!

Gaylord fastened his cases, carried them down into the hall. Then he slipped out of the back door. Mother would only find something to go on about if he stayed. He just didn't know what was the matter with her these days.

To a boy who was not only in love but who was also awakening to a complex and beautiful birthright, the morning was breathtakingly lovely. He wandered through the laden branches, the sun-dappled grass of the orchard, down to the river. He had a sad duty to perform: To pull his boat into the safety of the crumbling old shed that served as a boathouse. It would be Easter before he needed it again – half a year gone. Half a year before he once again trailed his hand in the cool water, or heaved at the oars, or ran a loving hand along the smooth paintwork.

But before he put the boat away for the winter he had another duty to perform: a pleasanter, though equally sad one.

During the night, between three and three thirty, he had been unable to sleep. Tossing and turning, trying desperately to see with his mind's eye the sweet face of his German love, he had had an idea so sudden, so beautiful, that it had moved him almost to tears. He would call his precious boat after his loved one. He would call it *The Christine*.

Had sleep not overtaken him he would have carried out his plan there and then. Nevertheless, as soon as breakfast was over he came up to his room and slipped the half bottle of lemonade from his bedside cupboard into his pocket.

And now, the moment had come. He walked along the landing stage until he stood over his boat. He took the bottle from his pocket. Holding it carefully in his handkerchief he smashed it against the boat. 'I name this vessel *The Christine*,' he cried in a loud but emotionally unsteady voice. 'God bless her, and all who sail in her.'

He stood in silence, deeply moved. Then he kneeled rather precariously on the rickety landing stage and began picking bits of broken glass out of the boat.

A feminine voice behind him said, 'Hello, Gaylord.'

It was a moment before he could turn, so delicately poised was he. Who was it? Either Amanda or young Liz, presumably, though it hadn't sounded quite like either of them.

He turned; and nearly lost his balance. It was Christine Haldt.

He rose to his feet, staring. Then, without taking his eyes off her face for a moment, he began to walk back along the landing stage. He was awestruck. He had a weird feeling that he had conjured her up with his little ceremony.

She was dressed in modern style. That is to say, she was wearing a frock of some drab, earth-coloured material that hung drearily down to her ankles (or in places her heels, the hemline verging on the erratic.) Hair and dark glasses covered everything of her features except a tip of nose and the curve of lips.

But she was beautiful – and unbelievable! To Gaylord she was as beautiful and unbelievable as Titania, La Belle Dame Sans Merci, the Lorelei. 'Christine!' he whispered as he trod precariously the rotting planks.

'Hello, Gaylord,' she said again, smiling at his surprise. She stood motionless, relaxed, her hands hanging still at her side.

He reached the bank, seized her shoulders, strove to kiss her, but with an age-old feminine movement she evaded his lips. 'Christine! What are you doing here? Have – you come back?'

'Come back? No, I do not go.'

'But – I saw you leaving for the airport.'

'Yes. So. But at the airport there is the usual English strike. We cannot fly. We return to the hotel. We are in dudgeon. But then–'

'Oh, there you are, Christine,' said a male voice. 'Hello, Pentecost.'

'Hello, Miles,' said Gaylord, without the enthusiasm with which he usually greeted his hero. There he'd been in a mood of near despair. Then, his dear Christine had appeared before him. Christine, whom he had thought a thousand miles away, changing his despair to an intensity of joy. And before he could even get the feeling of

228

joy properly into his system, before he'd even *kissed* his beloved, a third party had come crashing like a rhinoceros on to the scene. And for a moment the fact that the rhinoceros was Ex-Captain of the School, Ex-Captain of Cricket and Ex-Captain of Rugger seemed totally irrelevant.

Miles said, 'I know. Let's take your boat out, Pentecost. We were wondering what to do with ourselves, weren't we, Christine.'

Gaylord said, 'But I don't understand. I thought Christine was in Germany. And – Christine appeared, and then you. Had you come together, or–?'

'We cycled over to see you. But we met Amanda near the house, and she wanted to pin me down to marrying her on her eighteenth birthday. She says it's either me or the veil, and she much prefers me. Now you row, Pentecost, and Christine and I will steer.' He gave Gaylord his brilliant on off smile.

We cycled over to see you. It sounded horribly proprietorial. On the other hand, she apparently had wanted to come and see him. He still didn't understand. He turned to Christine. 'You mean – you're staying in England?'

She gave him a very gentle and loving smile. But before she could reply there was a further crashing through the undergrowth and Amanda appeared, panting. She took in the situation in a moment. 'Can I come?' she said.

'Does Mummy say you can?' asked Gaylord.

'Yes,' she said promptly. 'At least, I'm sure she would, it's just that I haven't asked her.'

'Sorry, Mandy,' said Gaylord. He didn't want to be difficult. But there had been an embargo on Amanda in boats ever since, early in the holidays, she had fallen in. And Gaylord wasn't taking any chances with his mother, at the moment. He was handling her like china.

'Can you wait while I go and ask her?' Amanda asked eagerly.

'Actually,' said Roger, treating Mandy to a most respectful smile, 'I haven't an awful lot of time. Tight schedule, and all that.'

Gaylord was a bit cross. A kid sister, suggesting a School Captain should waste his time waiting for her! 'Off you go, Mandy,' he said, kindly but firmly.

'Oh, all right,' said Amanda, sticking her lower lip out. She stomped off muttering. Men! She looked back. There was the river, cool, infinitely inviting. There were her two favourite males, strolling down to the landing stage with that German creature.

Roger and Christine were talking and laughing. Gaylord looked as though he was wondering why Fate, having decided to produce his beloved Christine out of a hat, as it were, had felt impelled to produce Roger Miles as well. Amanda thought how nice it would have been if she could have got the brace and bit from Gaylord's woodwork set, and drilled the boat full of holes before they embarked. Then she could have swam out and rescued dear Gaylord and darling Roger and put her foot on the German creature's head as she went down for the third time. But the plan was impracticable for two reasons: the others would be in the boat long before she could even get the brace and bit; and she'd lost her water wings.

Fate, however, came up with an alternative Plan which, though less comprehensive and certainly less dramatic, served to get *one* of her favourite men out of the Erl King's Daughter's clutches. As she approached the house her mother's face appeared at the window, her mother's voice called, 'Mandy, is Gaylord about? Tell him he's wanted on the telephone.'

'Whoopee!' cried Amanda, and tore off. By the time she reached the landing stage, Roger and Christine were already seated comfortably in the stern, and Gaylord was grasping the oars. 'Gaylord!' panted Amanda, clearly in the last stages of exhaustion. 'You're – wanted on the telephone. Mummy says it's terribly urgent and important.'

'Who is it?' said Gaylord, looking chagrined.

'Dunno. But I think it's from ever so far away. New Zealand or somewhere.'

'I don't know anyone in New Zealand,' said Gaylord.

Christine said, 'While you are saying, "I know no one in New Zealand," the cost of the call increases alarmingly.'

'Could be a New Zealand solicitor, to tell you a forgotten relative's left you a fortune,' pointed out Roger.

'Already the bill for the call will be many pounds,' said Christine.

'Off you go, old chap,' Roger said. 'I'll take the oars.'

'Thank you, Miles,' Gaylord said gratefully. He climbed out of the boat, stifling as unbearable the feeling that they were glad to see him go. He ran towards the house. Once he looked back. His beloved boat was in mid-stream, bearing the woman he loved and the man he most admired in the whole world. Yet, for some reason he could not define, this thought did not give him the pleasure it should have done.

His mind was also on the telephone call. It *couldn't* be New Zealand, of course, he told himself. But it would be jolly exciting if it were. He imagined himself saying casually at school: 'Had a call from New Zealand during the holidays. Clear as a bell.' Why, Roger Miles might even mention it to the fellows at Oxford. 'Friend of mine had a call from NZ the other morning. I happened to be round at his place, and–' He looked down at Mandy, running by his side. 'Are you *sure* it was New Zealand?'

'Not *sure*,' she panted. 'But it was something like that. Hemel Hempstead?' She suggested hopefully. And then she peeled off and went and lost herself in the stack yard. If as was always possible, she had slightly exaggerated the telephone call's importance, there would be much to be said for being absent when the inevitable inquest began.

And, sure enough, when Gaylord reached the house there was the telephone back on its hook and his mother looking vaguely surprised to see him. 'Hello, dear. Have you been running?'

'Telephone,' he gasped. 'Mandy said–'

'Oh, yes.' She remembered. 'Oh, it was only Liz Bunting. I said you might be some time, could *I* do anything, but she said it was nothing of importance.'

Gaylord felt very bitter. What did young Liz think she was playing at? There he'd been, all set to show his beloved *and* his dear friend how brilliantly he could handle a boat; all set to spend this lovely morning on the river with a beautiful girl and a handsome, delightful companion, all set to solve the mystery of Christine's return, and of her future plans. And young Liz spoils it all by telephoning – on a matter of no importance! And, he remembered, Amanda hadn't helped with her talk of New Zealand. 'Mandy's a little chump,' he said moodily. 'She said it was New Zealand.'

'Darling, you don't *know* anyone in New Zealand.'

'Haven't I got an Uncle Frank out there?' he remembered suddenly.

'Yes. But *he's* hardly likely to take it into his head to give you a ring. The only news he's ever had of you is a jolly little card with a stork and the words, "Welcome, Stranger!"'

'He *could* have,' Gaylord said, mooning round the kitchen, helping himself to raisins and sultanas.

May said, 'Goodness, you *have* got it on you. Go on. Go and play. I'm busy.'

Go and play! She couldn't have said anything more hurtful. Made him sound like a bally child. Suddenly he was no longer mooning round the kitchen. He dived for the back door, went out, slammed the door furiously behind him.

No one treated May like that. She went and wrenched open the back door. 'Gaylord! Come back!' It was an absolute command.

He came back, looked at her sheepishly. 'Now,' she said. 'Apologize for slamming that door. Then say goodbye properly.'

He stared down at the doorstep, looked up into his mother's face, didn't like what he saw, went back to studying the doorstep.

234

'Sorry, Mum,' he said.

'I should jolly well think so. Now off you go. Goodbye.'

'Goodbye.' He risked another glance at her face, hoping for one of her sudden grins. But her face remained cold. He wandered off. He heard the door shut behind him. And, alone in the kitchen, May was still not smiling. What had happened to her normally amiable son? He's still in love, she thought. Still in love with the Erl King's Daughter. Well, a term at school should settle that. If it didn't, she thought glumly, we're in for a Merry Christmas.

The door opened again. Gaylord edged in sheepishly. He gave his mother a sideways look. 'Sorry I was rude, Mum,' he said with a shy half smile.

'*That's* all right.' Impetuously she came and put her arm about his shoulders. 'What's the trouble, Gaylord?'

He was silent. Then he said, 'You remember that German girl? Christine?'

'Ye–es?' she said gravely, resisting a desire to point out that, even at her advanced age, she could remember things that happened a fortnight ago with some clarity.

'She's come back,' said Gaylord. 'At least – she never went.'

'Oh, *no*,' May said. 'Come back where?'

'Well, I don't know. She and Roger Miles

just turned up. They're out in my boat at present. I was going, only – Liz rang up.'

'Oh, poor old Gaylord.' She sensed something of what this must mean to him. How could she help? 'Look,' she said, 'would you like to ask them for lunch?'

'Oh, *please*, Mum. If it isn't any trouble.'

Why did *all* men, she wondered, assume it was possible to have two extra for lunch without any trouble. But she didn't say anything. She sensed that if Fräulein Haldt had turned up as it were from the dead, on the last day of the holidays, and promptly gone off with Roger Miles in Gaylord's boat, then Gaylord must be in grave need of a mother's care and protection.

He said, 'I'll go and see whether I can find them. Tell them about lunch.'

He went towards the door. He didn't think there was much chance of rejoining them. Thanks to spinneys and fences and tributary streams it wasn't possible to follow the river bank very far. Nevertheless, he'd do his best.

But he never even reached the back door. For it was flung open and Christine, a furious and dripping Rhine Maiden, plonked herself in the middle of the kitchen, while quite a lot of Trent poured from her and formed pools and rivulets and puddles and streams on May's kitchen floor. And in a loud voice cried, 'My God! Nearly do I lose my life.'

Phew! It's the last time I have an au pair girl, thought May. And to think I imagined she was safe in Germany. 'What happened, dear?' she asked, trying to keep it nice and English.

Christine said, 'We are approaching the rapids. And what does he do, the Dumm-kopf? He abandons his oars, in order that he may attempt to kiss me. And suddenly we are in the water, and–' she ran across to Gaylord, flung her dripping arms about him, pressed her wet cheek against him – 'Oh, my poor Gaylord, your boat, your beautiful boat–' Words failed her.

Gaylord's mouth was dry. 'What – about my boat?'

'Ruined, shattered beyond repair,' said Christine, wringing her hands.

Gaylord's wail of despair was worthy of Lear at his most harassed. He rushed outside. May, who had already flung a towel round Christine's shoulders, said 'Come on. Upstairs. I'll turn your bath on. Then I'll help you get out of those wet things.' And upstairs she said, 'what happened to Roger Miles? Is he all right?'

Christine waved a violent arm, nearly hitting May who was struggling with one of her zips. '*He* is all right. Because I rescue him. He, the great sportsman, the great Captain of this and that, does not swim! In

Germany, the young men all swim. But this Captain – I put my hand under his chin, I say, "Relax now, let your body go limp and I, Christine Haldt, will preserve you." But no. He threshes about like a distraught octopus, making the rescue operation difficult.'

'But he's safe? Will he come up to the house, do you think?'

'When I leave him,' Christine said disgustedly, 'he is vomiting up the river and the little fishes.'

'Oh. Poor Roger.' She remembered something. 'Did he really try to kiss you?'

'Yes. Oh, he is a nice young man. But I think perhaps he wishes to do more than kiss. This I do not like. I am virtuous.' She remembered something. 'Oh, when Gaylord wishes to hold my hand or even kiss me, I let him. It is sweet, he is so young, and I think maybe it gives him much pleasure. But this one, no. I think perhaps his intentions are not entirely honourable.'

May thought perhaps they weren't, either. She had long ago decided that Miles was a nice lad, but conceited, a bit of an ass, and basically untrustworthy. And if he really had wrecked Gaylord's boat, and if this helped her son to see the feet of clay inside the Hush Puppies, then she really would be rather relieved. 'Now have a good, long soak,' she said to Christine.

'Lunch about one. I'll find some clothes,'

and she came downstairs thinking: what can I give them all to eat at short notice, my father-in-law certainly won't relish ham and salad, and I hope to goodness Gaylord's got over his moods. Oh poor kid, if his boat really is broken, and what's all this about him kissing Christine? And this thought led on to thoughts of her son becoming enmeshed in another woman's toils, and of poor Liz Bunting so loyal and loving, and of how young *they* all seemed, and how old *she* seemed. And yet, and yet – were not the emotions that disturbed them still disturbing her? Was she not as eager and anxious about tonight's meeting with Charles, and about what the veiled easel held, as any girl? And she wondered what she could lend Christine to wear, and whether she had time to knock together a cheese soufflé.

Gaylord made a beeline for the river, and was not overjoyed when Amanda fell into step beside him. 'Gaylord, where are you going? Why are you in such a hurry? Gaylord, *was* it New Zealand on the telephone? I wondered afterwards, what language do they speak in New Zealand? Are Roger and Christine still on the river? Gaylord, wasn't it foul of Roger not to wait for me? I shouldn't have been long.'

They came to the river. Gaylord looked upstream, down stream. Both ways, the still

239

noontide dreamed. No boat, no Roger, no wreckage. But Gaylord knew in his heart where the answer would lie. He began to run downstream. Amanda went with him, her bright, narrow eyes occasionally glancing up to study her brother's face. She sensed something that was meat and drink to her: disaster!

And there, suddenly, walking towards them, was Roger Miles, a bundle of wet clothes under his arms, his shirt knotted tight about his middle. Amanda looked at his wet and naked figure with interest. 'Hello, Roger. You look like John the Baptist. Gaylord, doesn't he look like John the Baptist?'

Roger said, 'Hello, Mandy. Hello, Gaylord old chap. Er, afraid we had a spot of bother with that boat of yours.'

So it *was* true. 'Where is it?' said Gaylord.

Roger Miles nodded downstream. Gaylord began to run. Amanda said hopefully, 'If we waded into the river you could baptise me, Roger. I've *been* done, but this would be much jollier.'

Roger shook his head, and threw himself down on the grass. Amanda looked at him with concern. Roger wasn't being as much fun as usual. And it occurred to her that he had something on his mind. It also occurred to her that an hour ago he'd gone off in a boat with the German creature and now here he was disguised as the Baptist.

'Where's Miss Haldt?' she asked.

'In a steaming hot bath, I should imagine,' he said lugubriously.

Suddenly a great light dawned. A smile of ineffable bliss spread over Amanda's little face. But she spoke like one who scarcely dares to ask. 'I say, Roger? You – you *didn't* tip her in?'

Roger was silent. 'You *could* put it that way,' he said at last.

Amanda flung herself on her back. 'O frabjous day!' She kicked her legs in the air, pedalled an imaginary bicycle. 'Callooh! Callay!'

Then a thought struck her. She stopped pedalling, sat up, said in censorious tone, 'You didn't *rescue* her?'

Roger, omitting to point out that the boot had been on the other foot, nodded. 'You little beast,' he said. 'I couldn't let her drown.'

Amanda couldn't really see why not. Nevertheless, she knew you couldn't expect a man to have the same ruthless decisiveness as a woman. So she lay back again in the sunshine and said, 'Shall you expect me to go out to work when we're married, Roger darling?'

'Naturally. I don't intend to do a stroke.'

'Oh, good. I'll support you.' She was silent, pondering how she should support her beloved. Typing, needlework, writing novels?

She couldn't think of anything else. Yet there must be other things. She pondered further. Something else she'd heard of but she hadn't a clue what it meant. 'Roger?'

'Mmm?'

'What are immoral earnings?'

But at this moment Gaylord came striding along, threw himself down on the grass. 'It's aground,' he said in a flat voice. 'Below the weir. There's quite a hole in the bows.'

'Oh, Lord, I'm *sorry*,' Roger said dismally.

'That's all right,' said Gaylord.

They were all silent. 'It must be possible to mend it,' said Roger.

'Yes,' said Gaylord, who knew that, mended or not, it would never be the same.

'Some fresh timbers, a dash of paint. It'll be as good as new.'

'Yes.' said Gaylord. His new boat, named *The Christine*, with its sturdy timbers, its flawless paintwork – a repaired and repainted hulk! He didn't ever want to see it again.

'Needless to say, any expense–' said Roger. 'I mean, I know you'd have been in charge but for the telephone call. Nevertheless, in the circumstances–'

'That's all right, thank you, Miles,' said Gaylord. His boat, his pride and joy, smashed because his great friend had tried to kiss the girl he, Gaylord, loved. No. It *couldn't* have been that. Christine must have been mistaken. And yet he knew, in the sadness of his heart, that this morning three things dearest to him had been broken, or sullied, or endangered: a boy's boat, a boy's hero worship, a boy's first love. He said, 'Mother's invited you to lunch. I can lend you some clothes.'

'Thanks, old man. Did Christine – er – say anything?'

Gaylord was silent. Then, rather wearily, he got to his feet. 'Come on,' he said. 'I'll find you those clothes.'

CHAPTER 15

May was just taking the cheese soufflé out of the oven when Gaylord's voice said, 'Mum, Miles *can* stay for lunch while his clothes dry out?'

She straightened up, to see a very wet young man in very wet shirt and slacks, for Roger had been reluctant to appear before the elegant Mrs Pentecost clad only in a loincloth. Lord, the Erl King himself, she thought wildly. She said, 'Of course. I said so. Take him up and lend him some of your things. And get back as soon as you can. Time, tide and soufflés wait for no man.'

'I say, that's rather good, Mrs Pentecost,' Roger said appreciatively.

She gave him a cold look. He'd caused enough trouble for one morning, trying to get round Christine. He wasn't getting round her.

Five minutes later Gaylord and Roger came into the dining room. Gaylord said, 'We've put Miles' wet clothes in the scullery, with Christine's. That all right?'

'Yes,' said May, beginning to feel like a branch of the Shipwrecked Mariners' Society.

Christine came in, wearing a dress of May's. Immersion in a cold river, followed by a long hot bath, had given the German girl's complexion an almost ethereal purity. Her still wet hair, caught in a yellow ribbon, gleamed. Gaylord thought he had never seen anyone or anything as beautiful and desirable. In fact the eyes of all the men strayed to her, instinctively, time and time again. But she did not look up and meet their gaze. She stayed demure, immersed in her own thoughts.

May, seeing the scarcely veiled disgust with which Grandpa was poking at his helping of soufflé, said: 'I'm sorry lunch isn't up to standard, Father-in-law, but we had a slight contretemps.'

Christine shot a quick glance at her hostess. Eine Katastrophe! And these English called it 'a slight contretemps'. They hadn't even got a word in their own language

244

for it, apparently.

She was no longer demure. She glared at May, then round the table. 'A contretemps? I, Christine Haldt, am subjected to un-welcome attentions, and immersed in the stream. And, worst of all, my poor Gaylord's boat is destroyed.' And she rose from the table, went and leaned over Gaylord, and rubbed her cheek sympathetically against his. She lifted her face, gazed around the table. 'He is like a child with a broken toy.' She went back to rubbing cheeks. 'Are you not, *mein Liebchen?*'

'No. Not really,' said Gaylord, a bit muffled.

Christine went back to her seat. But she eyed the assembled English sternly. 'All this,' she said. 'And you call it "a slight contretemps".'

The English look duly sheepish at this reproof. All except Grandpa, who said. 'Excellent soufflé, May. Why on earth don't you give it us more often?'

May said, 'Because you look hurt and aggrieved if I don't give you red meat twice a day.'

'Make me sound like a tiger in a zoo,' said Grandpa, not displeased by this compliment to his masculine common sense. But Jocelyn said, 'What is this about your boat, Gaylord?'

Gaylord didn't want to talk about it. 'It's

got a bit damaged,' he said, staring at his plate.

'Oh, Lord. I *am* sorry.'

'It went right over the weir,' said Amanda.

'How on earth did you manage that?' said Jocelyn, who had refused to buy Gaylord a boat until he was thoroughly competent to handle one. He saw, too late, that his wife was giving him warning looks.

Amanda said, 'It wasn't him. He *was* going, but then somebody rang him up from New Zealand, so Roger and Miss Haldt took the boat and Miss Haldt went and fell into the water and Roger dived in and saved her but even he couldn't save the boat as well and it went over the weir.' She gave Roger a devastating smile and Miss Haldt a look of scarcely diluted venom.

At this travesty of the facts Christine remained silent, Roger made to speak and thought better of it, May thought well surely Roger isn't going to let that pass, and Jocelyn said, 'New Zealand? Whom do we know in New Zealand?'

But John Pentecost was remembering something. He slipped into his courteous old English gentleman act, and, fairly wrapping Christine in grandfatherly concern, said, 'Did you say something about "unwelcome attentions", my dear?'

'It was nothing,' said Christine.

The old gentleman asked, sotto voce,

'Young Gaylord not been trying any hanky panky, I hope?'

Christine looked amused. 'Gaylord? No, he is sweet. He is not yet of an age to pay unwelcome attentions.'

Since Grandpa's voice, even when sotto, had a good decibel rating, Gaylord heard this exchange in its entirety. And was so hurt and incensed that he muttered, 'Excuse me,' and left the room.

'What's up with him?' demanded Grandpa.

'Just puberty,' said Jocelyn, smiling.

'Puberty?'

'Yes.'

Grandpa reached for the wine bottle, filled Jocelyn's glass. 'Never had it in my day,' he said. '*We* just grew up. Made life a lot simpler, I must say.'

But despite Gaylord's exit, the emotional crisis continued. For Christine now fixed a baleful glance on Roger Miles and hissed, 'Low down heel!' She turned to May and asked, quietly, 'My English idiom is correct?'

'American slang, really,' murmured May. 'But it will do.'

Roger looked startled, Jocelyn intrigued. Grandpa sank back with a low purr of contentment. He liked a girl of spirit, and from what he'd seen of this young fellow it wouldn't hurt him to be taken down a peg or two.

But Amanda was on her feet immediately.

'How dare you call Roger a low-down heel?'

Christine too sprang to her feet. She pointed a denunciatory finger at Roger. 'Because he *is* a low-down heel. There you sit,' she cried. 'While Gaylord is accused, when all the time it is you who engage in the hanky panky. And you let it be said by this – this *infant* that it is *you* who rescue *me* from drowning – *me*, Christine Haldt, whose swimming was the wonder of the Gymnasium.'

'Don't call me an infant,' cried Amanda.

Jocelyn said, 'Amanda! Sit down! How dare you speak to a guest in that way?' He glanced at Christine, and was gratified to see a look of approval on her face.

Roger Miles stood up. 'Mrs Pentecost, it was most kind of you to give me lunch. But I have a rather tight schedule, so if I might keep this shirt and trousers for the time being I will take myself and my wet clothes off your hands.' He flashed her his brilliant smile.

She smiled back. She was, she knew, a sucker for good manners.

Roger said, 'And if you would be kind enough to allow Christine to accompany me in your borrowed clothes, I will see that they are cleaned and returned promptly.'

'Of course,' said May. Everybody rose. Christine said, 'And you do not mind that I borrow your beautiful clothes, Mrs Pentecost?'

May said, 'That's all right. But – I still don't understand. I'd imagined you were in Germany.'

'No. It is the English strikes. We–'

'Please excuse us,' said Roger, glancing at his watch. 'Come, Christine.'

They went. Gaylord, hidden in the long grass of the orchard, watched them go. He longed to run after them, to say 'Goodbye Christine, shall I see you again, how long are you staying?' even to utter that sad, despairing valediction: 'Remember me!' But he couldn't. *They* were together. In spite of her anger with Miles over his behaviour in the boat, they were together and apparently friendly. And she was presumably staying in Roger's father's hotel until the strike ended. It seemed to Gaylord to have the inevitability of Greek tragedy. How *could* two such wonderful people, thrown together by Fate, fail to fall in love? There was certainly no blame for them in Gaylord's heart.

They mounted their bicycles, pedalled away in the quiet afternoon. He watched them till they were out of sight. Miles he would see at Christmas. He thought it unlikely he would ever see Christine again.

And there was another Christine also lost to him, for he would never sail in her after this morning's disaster.

He wandered, hands stuffed into his pockets, down towards the weir. The river ran faster here, until it widened into a dark, smooth pool where the first leaves of autumn drifted aimlessly like Chinese junks. Here the water lay, gathering its power. Then, suddenly, it was over the weir like a springing tiger, joyous, tumultuous. And below the weir, on a little sandy shore, lay The Christine. She lay on her side, the water lapping at her hull, and trickling dismally into her scuppers through a hole in her bows.

Gaylord ran down the bank. The boat had come to rest in one of his favourite places, this sheltered cove he had known all his life, a place of picnics in high summer, cooled by the tumbling waters, made drowsy by the sound of the weir – a place of lonely thoughts in winter dusks, with the mists stealing about the river meadows, unquiet ghosts, and the lights of home hazy in the distance.

He went down on his knees to examine the boat. The oars had gone. The timber he had painted with his own hand was torn and jagged. A tiny sound came from the scuppers. A minnow, eyes starting and desperate, threshed about in the inch of muddy water, scales flashing grey and silver. Death was coming for him; and he, who had no concept of death, knew it, and was afraid.

Gaylord, growing up, knew that he and this little creature, in some way he could not define, shared a common being. They were one, as he and the stars and the autumn crocuses were one, all part of the pattern, all part of a passing thought in the mind of God, he wondered, for though he was growing up he was young, and such images came easily to him. Or were they, perhaps, one only because they were both a part of the world's suffering? Was the minnow, struggling with a disaster he could not comprehend, simply a symbol of his own bemused state?

Hands infinitely gentle with compassion, he scooped up the minnow, and lowered it carefully into the stream. It dived down into the muddy bottom, unsurprised, unthankful; for, since it had not been thought necessary to equip minnows with a memory, his life and death struggle had already ceased to be a part of him.

Gaylord stood for a long time staring into the moving water, vicariously enjoying the little fish's regained freedom, forgetting for a moment, in that sharing, his own loneliness and loss – boat gone, summer gone, holidays over, Christine gone – and – dare he admit it–? his admiration for his hero ever so slightly tarnished.

He looked again at his boat. Then he resolutely turned his eyes from it and climbed the bank, and went to the old barn, where he found a large can of liquid, and old tractor tyre, and a pile of yellowing newspapers.

An idea was forming...

CHAPTER 16

'Gosh, Mum, you do look super,' said Gaylord.

'Do I, dear?' said May. She was encouraged. A woman who could draw cries of admiration from her own son couldn't look too bad. And now here come Jocelyn to add to the applause. 'Hello, old girl. Glad you've put a long skirt on. Suits you.'

'Thanks, darling.'

He looked at her hair. 'Good Lord, you've gone blue.'

'Don't you like it?'

'Yes. It's just–'

'What? Jocelyn, say what you have to say.'

'It's – is it that stuff from Boots, Gaylord was talking about?'

'No, you fool. It's just a new rinse. *Blue Heaven.*'

'Very nice too.'

She gave up. She would never know what he really thought. But *she* liked it. She wondered whether Charles would notice.

She saw her father-in-law eyeing her with considerable approval, and was pleased. The old man was a great admirer of good-looking, well-turned-out women. *And* she sensed that, for him, one of the advantages of age was that he could stare at such a woman with frank and open admiration, and not give offence. He said, 'You look simply splendid, May. Have a nice evening.'

She grinned. 'You don't look so bad yourself, old man.'

He didn't either. His moustache was clipped with precision. His hair was neat, his fresh complexion newly shaved. A generation, she thought, who went to the trouble to make the best of themselves. And he was only staying at home. She looked at Jocelyn. Much more casual. A loose-fitting body in loose-fitting clothes. Hair a bit awry. But attractive. Definitely attractive. Seven out of ten for getting an effect without really trying.

Then she looked at her son. 'Gaylord! You can't come in denims.'

He looked uncomfortable. 'Do you mind awfully if I don't come? I want to have a look at my boat.'

'But it will be dark soon.'

'I can use a torch.'

'And Mr Bunting *did* ask you.'

Gaylord's heart sank even lower, if possible. He knew that, if mother had made up her mind that he was going, she would produce counter arguments, patiently and reasonably, until she wore him down. Few men had the tenacity to counter such feminine determination, certainly not Gaylord.

But then support came from a surprising quarter. Jocelyn said, 'It's his last evening, May. Let him do what he wants.'

'Good Lord, he's not going to execution.' said May. But she usually listened to Jocelyn when he *did* intervene. 'Well, if Charles won't think it rude–?'

'I don't suppose he'll even notice,' said Jocelyn.

'Right ho, Gaylord,' said May. 'But don't be late in.'

'Thanks, Mum.' He slipped away, as unobtrusive as a snake in the grass.

'Now,' said May. 'As soon as Amanda condescends to put in an appearance we can go.'

And Amanda appeared – in a frilled party frock down to her ankles, and with her hair framing her face in two short plaits. She looked beautiful, and she knew it. She was as pleased with herself as a butterfly in the sunlight. May examined her daughter for lipstick, eye shadow, and nail varnish, and found none. But how long, she wondered, before she starts to try it on, and I have to decide at what point I let her begin to grow up. Lord, don't let it be yet, she thought. Spare us, O Lord, the innocence of our children.

But on the drive into Ingerby her mind came back to the subject that had occupied it for so long.

Charles was in love with her. Charles had worked on a portrait of her. Now he had asked her, and her family, to an unveiling.

Of what? Of whom? The Mayoress of Ingerby? A view of the Town Hall, commissioned for the Municipal Art Gallery? Or of Mrs Jocelyn Pentecost?

She had to admit that the last was the most likely. And if it was–! To be loved by a famous artist, to be painted by him–? It was an honour that fell to few women. Saskia was the only one she could think of at the moment. Of course, it was nothing to be proud about. It was just that – here, in her heart, she would carry a warmth; a secret, proud, joyful warmth that she would take to the grave. A warmth that no one, not even her dear Jocelyn, would ever suspect. And bully for me, she suddenly thought. But what about Charles? *What* secret warmth was *he* going to carry to the grave? The knowledge that he had loved, and once kissed, another man's wife (*and* had his face slapped for it)? No. Poor old Charles, she began to realize, had had a pretty poor life of it, since the tragedy of Rachel's death.

And she could do nothing to help him. Her woman's heart and body were capable of infinite comfort, infinite consolation. But not for Charles. Only for one man, to whom she belonged like a chained bear, to whom she was bound by law and custom and above all love. Because of these dear chains she could show Charles neither love nor compassion. Jocelyn's claims were absolute. Jocelyn was a kindly, unselfish, generous man. Yet in this case custom – honour even – demanded that he behave like a Shylock.

And Jocelyn, she thought, accepted this role smugly and unthinkingly. Sitting there beside him, in the dusk of the car, she felt a most unusual irritation with her husband. She said, very quietly, 'I should like to comfort old Charles.'

'What's that, May?' His eyes were on the road.

She said, still quietly. 'I should like to comfort Charles.'

He drove on in silence. Then he said, equally quiet, 'How do you mean? Comfort him?'

'As one comforts a child,' she said.

The car drew up at an amber light. The light changed to red. 'Hold him to my heart,' she said.

Red-amber. Green. The car didn't move. 'Green, Daddy,' hissed Amanda from the back seat; aware, to her chagrin, that a sotto voce, and therefore almost certainly fascinating, conversation was taking place on the front seat.

The car surged forward. 'Funny thing to say,' said Jocelyn. She was silent. He said, 'Yes. Nice of you, May. See your point. But–?

Think he'd misinterpret your motives.'

'Yes,' she said sadly. 'I suppose he would.'

'Could be very embarrassing for him, May.'

'Of course.'

They were at the next lot of traffic lights. Jocelyn waited for the lights to change. Then he delivered judgement. 'Don't think it would work, old girl. After all, you can't just throw your arms round a chap, can you? I mean, I don't need to say I'm not jealous or anything. But – well, you can't, can you?'

When they reached Ingerby May said, 'Let's drive round a bit. We're early, and I'm nervous.'

'You? Nervous? Why?'

'There's quite a chance it's I who am going to be unveiled.'

'Oh, shouldn't think so, old girl.' Nevertheless, he drove once round the square and then into *The Swan* car park. And May had been right. They *were* early. When they entered the Trent Room there were only Charles and two waiters.

They went in a little apprehensively. Despite Charles' invitation, their last encounter had been fraught, and Charles was an unpredictable blighter, anyway. The fact that his invitation had sounded warm was little to go by.

But he advanced on them beaming, holding out his hands to May, most respectfully kissing her cheek, shaking hands with Jocelyn. 'My dear May, my dear Jocelyn, thank you for coming. Hello, young Amanda.'

May, remembering her feeling in the car, thought, Good old Charles. He's putting on a very fine show. Looking at him now, you'd never realize what a lonely man he really is.

Charles' exhibition was still on. The walls of the Trent Room were hung with his pictures. Jocelyn looked at them with interest, Amanda with boredom. But all May's attention was on a large picture on an easel in the middle of the room, loosely covered with a dustsheet. What did that rather drab dustsheet hide? She said, 'Gaylord asked to be excused, Charles.'

'I know. He rang up and apologized. Nice manners, that lad.'

May purred. It was good to know that all one's efforts bore a little fruit. But now Amanda was saying, 'That lady in that picture's purple, Mr Bunting.'

'Why shouldn't she be?' asked Charles, touchy immediately.

'Well, *I've* never seen a lady *that* colour.'

May thought, Oh Lord, the good impression made by one of my family is soon being ruined by another member. But Charles just looked thoughtfully at Amanda and said mildly, 'Now what can I get you all to drink?'

This was a new Charles. Courtesy and

258

Charles seldom went together. Yet here he was, his wolfish face suffused, not only with blue and purple bruising, but also with bonhomie and – could it be happiness? No, decided May. Not happiness. There could be no happiness for Charles. But Charles was a man of parts. And if, for once in his life, he decided on social élan, then he could be relied upon to do it properly.

'Awfully nice of you to ask us,' said Jocelyn. 'In view of–'

'My dear chap, I got just what I deserved. Now, where is everybody?' he waved a vague hand towards the veiled picture. 'If they don't come soon it'll be time for the ceremony. Now, sherry? Gin and whatever?'

They took their drinks. People began to arrive. Charles greeted them all with tremendous aplomb. May, hearing frequent references to Muhammad Ali, saved by the bell, and other jocular references to the ring, expected Charles' bonhomie to wither like the rose. But it didn't. Charles put on a very courageous act of being on top of the world.

May said to Jocelyn, 'Good Lord, Liz isn't here. Charles,' she called, 'Where's Liz?'

'She's coming with the others,' he called back.

What others? She wondered.

May sipped her gin and tonic, and made herself prowl round the pictures. But they did not interest her. What interested her was that shrouded picture on the easel; and the assured, apparently *happy* man chatting so easily with his guests. Why, after that one friendly greeting he'd scarcely looked in her direction. Yet how often, in other days, had she looked up in a crowded room to find his eyes fixed broodingly on her. Clearly, he was determined never to put a foot wrong again as far as she was concerned. She was really rather sorry. Or could it be, she wondered uneasily, that painting her portrait had got her out of his system. She did hope not. Frankly, she didn't think she wanted Charles to get her out of his system.

Amanda sipped her Coke and wished Liz would come. She, too, was fascinated to see what was under that dustsheet, to see whether Mr Bunting had made Mummy as fierce and stern as she really was. But until the picture was unveiled, she was bored. When you are ten, there is a limit to the attractions of grown-up conversation, a glass of Coke, and purple ladies.

She wondered whether she might manage a peep. She began to edge through the forest of legs towards the easel.

Now she was there. And no one, so far as she could tell, was looking. She put out a hand, took hold of a corner of the dustsheet, and was just bending down to peer under and up when a gentleman carrying four sherries without a tray (held reverently before him like the sacred chalice) stumbled into her, and the dust sheet began to slide very gently down off the portrait. Charles, with a wild cry of 'Goats and monkeys!' tore across the room and clamped the dustsheet and the top of the frame together with a strong hand. But the damage was done. One corner of the picture had been revealed – a vague background, a strand of woman's hair, a woman's shoulder.

'I'm ever so sorry,' said Amanda.

Charles gave her a look, but said, very gently, 'Think nothing of it, dear child. For a member of the Pentecost family your behaviour is surprisingly innocuous.'

'What's innocuous? said Amanda with interest. But Charles, still holding the dust-sheet in precarious position like a pre-Raphaelite water goddess her bath towel, called out, 'Ladies and Gentlemen, I had intended to wait for my daughter and the other guests. But they are late and my hand has been forced. We will proceed with the unveiling.'

There was a ripple of clapping, laughter and cheering.

Charles said, 'You may not agree. But personally I regard this as my major work. What Mona Lisa was to Leonardo, what Saskia was to Rembrandt, so – and I say this in all humility – so is this to me.'

There was a sharp intake of breath. He'd got their interest all right. And they were intrigued. Proud and touchy though old Charles was, he was a modest chap where his work was concerned. He knew his place in the long and noble history of art, and regarded it as a comparatively lowly one. So if he said this was something special, then it must be.

But May found herself trembling. She felt almost faint. And now Charles was looking round the room, saying, 'But I can't unveil my own work. 'Twouldn't be proper. We want a lady.' His eye fell on May. 'May, will you do it?'

'Oh, no,' she whispered. 'Oh, *no*.'

'Go *on*,' said Jocelyn, and with a hand under her elbow he steered her across the room.

Charles put a string into her hand. 'If you pull this something ought to happen. Unless young Amanda's fouled up the mechanism.'

I don't want to, thought May. I don't want these people to know what he thinks of me, *how* he sees me; it's private, it's almost indecent. I don't want to. Nevertheless she pulled the cord.

The sheet fell away – to reveal – to a burst of applause – a magnificent study of a lady in a crimson ball gown, seated on a high-backed, gilded chair. And it was some seconds before May realized that the lady was Frau Haldt, mother of Christine.

May stared, and stared. She swallowed. Then she said, generously, 'It's the best thing you've ever done, Charles.'

'*I* think so. Still, you couldn't go wrong with a subject like her. She's superb.'

'Yes. But – when did you do it?'

'They've been staying here, you know. Because of the strike. She sat for me for hours and hours.'

'Really?' *What* had she wanted to do? Comfort him like a child? She began to wonder whether Charles had found his own comfort.

But suddenly the enormity of his behaviour struck her. She began to laugh. She went on laughing. He looked rather hurt. 'What's the matter?'

'Oh, Charles. You *are* a tactless blighter.'

He looked even more hurt. He was damned sure no one ever thought him tactless before. He searched his conscience. And said, appalled, 'Good Lord, you mean Renate might not like me asking you to unveil her picture. I – just didn't think.'

She went on laughing. He said, uneasily, 'That *is* what you meant?'

'Partly,' she said, teasing.

'What else?'

'Nothing,' she said. 'Nothing at all, Charlie boy.'

He looked relieved. But now three more people came into the room. Liz Bunting, who gave May a tense smile; Christine Haldt, who

263

gave May a very self-possessed one; and Frau Renate Haldt who looked superb.

And the moment Renate Haldt entered the room it was clear that she saw no one but Charles; and that he saw no one but her. And they walked towards each other like two lovers meeting on a lonely shore, who see neither sun nor sea nor sky, but only the light shining from the face of the loved one. And Frau Haldt lifted her hand, and Charles brushed it with his lips, with a murmur of 'gnädige Frau'. And they stood, smiling at each other, the world forgetting.

So surprising, so moving, was this scene that it was followed by complete silence. Then there was an outburst of slightly embarrassed clapping, and nervous laughter.

Then Frau Haldt's mood changed. 'Who has unveiled my portrait?' she asked coldly.

Amanda said bravely, 'I started it. And Mummy finished it.'

'Indeed?' Fray Haldt looked at her with the same amusement she had shown on the doorstep. 'You seem to be a young lady who sets things in motion.'

'Is that good?' said Amanda.

But Frau Haldt had remembered something. 'Mrs Pentecost, that little picture Charles was doing of you, the nice Hausfrau one.'

May glanced at the crimson gown that so dominated the room from its easel. 'The

264

one where I look like a Brueghel peasant?'
she suggested amiably.

'No, no, my dear. You look very English
and – gemütlich. But I was going to say, I
will not let Charles forget it. I will see he
finishes it, you can rely on me.'

'Too kind,' murmured May.

Frau Haldt bowed to her in the friendliest
possible way, and went off to speak to
Charles. May's acknowledgement was no less
friendly. But flabbergasted would not be too
strong a word to describe her feelings. Well!
she thought. Talk about off with the old love
and on with the new! Charles certainly didn't
waste any time. *She sat for me for hours and
hours.* And I bet she didn't land him one if he
made advances, she thought unkindly.

She went and found Jocelyn. He gave her
his slow, loving smile. *Dear* Jocelyn! Finding
him, in this crowded room, was like slipping
into an old coat, or stepping across one's
own threshold after a long journey. He said,
'Beautiful woman, that Frau What's-her-
name. But–' he lowered his voice. 'You
know, May, it wouldn't surprise me if old
Charles hasn't gone and fallen for her.'

'Of course he has, you chump,' she said
fondly. 'Hook, line and sinker.'

'Good Lord,' said Jocelyn. He pottered
off. May saw Liz Bunting watching her
rather hopefully. She looked at Liz's pretty,
sad little face. She said, 'Gaylord's back at

school tomorrow, Liz. Why not come back with us? We'll have a late supper, and Jocelyn will run you home in the morning.'

'Thank you, Mrs Pentecost,' said Liz. 'I'd love to come.'

Jocelyn was a great believer in masterly inactivity, especially when the person required to be masterly inactive was himself.

Nevertheless, there were very rare occasions when he distrusted the course events were taking so much that he *did* interfere, usually as much to his own surprise as to everybody else's.

So after a time he winkled Frau Haldt out of a small group, steered her to a quiet corner of the room, and said, 'I'm a very old friend of Charles'. I just wanted to say how much I like your portrait.'

'That is most kind of you, Herr Pentecost. You see, I remember you well.'

'Thank you. Mrs Haldt, forgive my mentioning this, but Christine always spoke as though she lived in a Bavarian Castle with her parents and her grandfather.'

She gave him a long, cool look. 'No, Herr Pentecost. She does live in a Bavarian Schloss, where there is a grandfather and a Herr Baron, and a Baronin. But they are not her parents. She lives with me, her widowed mother, and I am the housekeeper, comptroller, chatelaine. We've no other relations.'

'So Christine–?' he said.

'Has invented her own family.'

'I see,' he said slowly. 'Onkel Willi? Aunt Ulrike? Prince von Bismarck?'

'Yes. And the Grandfather. A fine man. His word is law.'

Suddenly she was laughing. 'Oh, Herr Pentecost, it is not so terrible, is it?' Then she was serious again. 'So you see, Herr Pentecost, you do not need to protect your friend from me.'

'I'm sorry,' he said. Suddenly he liked her. He liked her daughter. They had style, both of them. Considerable style.

He went back to May. 'She's a widow,' he said.

'Who is?'

'Frau Haldt.'

'Great Scott, I never thought of that. How do you know?'

'I asked her.'

'Oh, Jocelyn, *darling*.' And now she did pull him to her and press her head against his chest, and her laughter rang out across the astonished room.

CHAPTER 17

Gaylord wandered out into the soft, September night, to put his dramatic plan into action. To destroy symbolically (though not in fact. That could never be) the bitter events of this morning. But somehow the ardent mood had evaporated. He just felt listless.

He tried to get himself back into the mood by thinking of his sorrows. Early tomorrow he would go back to school. Things would be different at school without Miles, but he didn't really think he'd miss him very much. And Miles would be here until the Oxford term began. Christine might be here, too. They would be together, enjoying themselves. Why, he supposed that if anyone mentioned the name of Gaylord Pentecost in a month's time, she'd have to make an effort to remember who he was.

And Gaylord Pentecost looked at himself coldly and clearly, and was appalled by what he saw. Did he see a lover, driven half mad by separation that might well last forever? Did he see a spurned and wretched lover, weeping with shame and anger? Did he see a lover, crazed with jealousy? Would he have Roger Miles 'nine years a-killing'? Certainly not. On the other hand, was he distressed, sad even, that he and Miles had reached the parting of the ways? No. The fact was that he felt nothing. He was completely empty, finished. His life, in its seventeenth year, had fizzled out like a damp firework. Nothing mattered, not love nor friendship nor jealousy nor time past, nor time present and to come. What a cold, unnatural creature he must be, to feel nothing when any normal person would be consumed by love, jealousy, hate, sorrow!

He went and looked at *The Christine*. Surely that wreck would stimulate him into some emotion!

The boat lay on its side in the darkness. It was smashed. Full stop.

The boat that brought him so much joy in the bright mornings, so much peace in the quiet evenings, the boat that he had named after his lovely girl, that had been the scene of Roger's attempted betrayal. It lay on its side in the darkness. It was broken. Full stop.

To feel nothing when you should be feeling some of the most violent emotions known to man is not only disturbing. It is very disappointing. He *would* make himself feel something. His plan, by its very drama, would purge his soul.

He hurried back to the old barn, went in, switched on the dim light.

He poked about hurriedly among the

potatoes and swedes and farming implements. He seized the old tractor tyre, snatched up a bundle of newspapers, the can of paraffin. He went back to *The Christine.*

He dragged and pushed the boat until it was almost floating. Then he chucked the newspapers into the boat, threw the tractor tyre on the top of them, poured the paraffin over the whole boat, dropped a lighted match on to the newspapers, and, with a mighty heave, shoved the boat into midstream.

It was magnificent. *The Christine* was immediately a floating pyre, flaming and spurting and hissing, sending up a great cloud of black smoke, a spurt and flurry of sparks to jig and dance impudently with the stars. Slowly, majestically, it moved down the river. Gaylord watched it. His eyes glinted in the now bright, now murky, flames. But they shone with another light. He was entranced. Bonfire Night was never like this! At the passing of the boat trees, hedges were illuminated, faded back into the darkness of the country night. The very water seemed ablaze. Birds lodged irritable complaints. A horse whinnied in fear.

Gaylord wanted to shout, to declaim, to sing at the top of his voice. And could think of nothing appropriate. The occasion demanded Wagner, obviously. Wagner must have written just the thing for this. But Gaylord could only think of the Prize Song from Die Meistersinger. So he sang that until his voice broke in sudden tears.

A concerned voice said, 'I say, Pentecost, you haven't gone potty or anything, have you?'

He had been staring so hard at the flames that he couldn't see a thing. But he knew the voice. 'Hello, Miles,' he said, trying desperately to keep his voice steady.

Miles said, 'That isn't your boat, is it?'

'Yes.'

'Oh, Lord. It only wanted a few planks.' He looked at Gaylord anxiously. 'What was on your mind? A Viking funeral?'

'Sort of.'

'You know, young Pentecost, I've sometimes thought you take life too seriously.'

Gaylord was silent. 'But you wanted something from Götterdämmerung,' said Miles. 'Meistersinger's no good.'

'I couldn't think of anything.'

They were both watching the boat as they talked, their eyes drawn instinctively to the glare in the enveloping dark. All Gaylord wanted was to be left alone; to watch the pyre of his life drifting away through the darkness. But Miles said, 'Er – Pentecost, old man?'

'Yes?' he said, eyes still on *The Christine*. She was still burning merrily, and had almost reached the place where the road and river ran together.

'I met Gibson for a bit of a conference.

There's quite a bit of handing over, you know. He said he thought he might try you for the XV, in the three-quarter line.'

Gaylord's senses reeled. The thought of the retiring, and the new, Captains of Rugger discussing *him* was intoxicating. The thought of being tried for the XV – there was no words to express it. 'Thanks, Miles,' he muttered. It was all he could manage.

For perhaps the first time in his life – certainly the first time Gaylord had ever heard him – Miles sounded slightly embarrassed. 'Thought I'd like to tell you myself,' he said. 'In view of – the boat and – everything.'

'Thanks, Miles,' said Gaylord. And to think that, half an hour ago, he had been doubting the very existence of friendship!

Miles said, 'There *is* something else, Pentecost. You know Christine – that German girl?' he reminded his friend.

'Yes,' said Gaylord in a tight voice. The flames were dying down a bit now. But it was still a good blaze. It had not, however, done anything for him. Except that, while before he had felt drained and empty he now felt his whole being knotted tight with emotions he could neither disentangle nor understand.

Miles said, 'Well, not a word to anyone. Especially her mother. But – well, we're sort of engaged.'

'Who are?' Gaylord said dully.

'Christine and I. You know. The German

girl. But it's a dead secret. I've got a lot of work to do on her mother, first. She thought I was a bellhop.'

'Who did?'

'Christine's mother.'

'I don't know her.'

''Course you do. She's Mr Bunting's latest.' He laughed. 'You ask your mother.'

'What do you mean, "you ask your mother"?'

'Oh, no offence, old chap. It's just that Amanda's saying there's a triangle situation between your parents and Bunting. I mean, nowadays, let's face it, these things happen–'

First, he had been empty and drained. Then emotions held him like the knotted muscles of cramp. Now, suddenly, the knots tightened excruciatingly. He flung himself at Miles, flailing, pummelling. 'Here, steady on, Pentecost,' cried Miles, going down before the onslaught. And now Gaylord was on top of him, thumping away at his chest. 'Take that back,' he was saying through clenched teeth. 'Take that back.'

'Take what back?'

'About my mother and Mr Bunting.'

'Oh, go to hell,' said Miles, heaving Gaylord off him. But Gaylord would not let go. They flayed savagely about on the gravel and finally, still in a tight embrace, rolled into the river.

It was Miles' head which went under first.

Gaylord seized his advantage, drew back his fist, and hit Miles very hard on the side of the jaw as he came up gasping.

Miles stopped gasping. He went limp. Gaylord stood up, seized his hero by the ankles, dragged him out of the water and laid him on the little beach. Miles lay like one dead. But his lips moved. 'That was a damned cowardly attack, young Pentecost.'

'It wasn't really, Miles,' said Gaylord reasonably, squatting on his haunches beside the body. 'Look, will you be all right? There's a fire engine and some car headlights on the river road. I think perhaps I ought to explain things a bit.'

He hurried off, across fields and fences and hedges, a little apprehensive. His boat was burning low on the water now, close to where road and river met. On the road the headlights of a car illuminated a large red fire engine, whose blue lights flashed eerily in the night. A searchlight from the fire engine shone upon *The Christine*, and, as Gaylord watched, a great jet of water hit his boat with a tremendous hissing and spluttering. Oh, dear, thought Gaylord. I seem to have started something. He did deplore the way the adults so often *over*-reacted to his little fancies.

May and Jocelyn, with Liz and Amanda on the back seat, came to the river road.

It seemed to May that the darkness was lit,

not only by their headlights, but by a dull glow on their right.

'Stop for a minute, darling,' she said. 'And switch your lights off.'

He did so. May shut her eyes tight for a few seconds. Then she opened them.

The glow came from the river. And it was bright now. It was an island of flame, drifting majestically down the stream.

Amanda was first out of the car, and down at the water's edge. But May and Liz were very close seconds. Amanda was dancing about with excitement. 'Mummy, it's Gaylord's boat. What do you think happened? It's super, isn't it? But where's Gaylord?'

Where *was* Gaylord? His boat was sailing down the river in flames. And he – disillusioned in friendship, disappointed in love – where was he? Half the earth was in shadow. All May knew was that he was somewhere in that shadow. Even a mother could not search a million miles of darkness. Unless– She stared, fascinated, at the boat. No. She was a sensible woman, with a sensible son. She could, thank God, devise no theory that could place Gaylord in that boat.

But now there was a banshee wailing in the night. White lights probing the darkness, blue lights flashing with patient irritability, were approaching. The wailing rose to an unbearable crescendo. The fire engine, and a red jeep, stopped beside them. The noise

275

mercifully ceased. In the sudden silence she could hear the crackling of the fire.

Men poured from the fire engine, ran out hoses. One of the men came across to them. 'I'd imagined it would be a cabin cruiser. But it's a rowing boat, isn't it?'

'That's right,' said May. 'It belongs to our son.'

The man gave her a sharp look. 'Have you any idea how a *rowing* boat could get into *that* state?'

Jocelyn said, 'With the Vikings, it was a form of – cremation. But–?'

'But there aren't many Vikings hereabouts, you were going to say, sir?'

'Not nowadays,' agreed Jocelyn.

'Hello, Mum,' said a rather wary voice.

'Gaylord!' cried Amanda. 'What's happened? Did you have to leap in to avoid the flames?'

'Hello, Gaylord,' Liz said quietly. She was awfully afraid she might faint from the relief of finding he was safe. But she was made of better stuff than that.

'Gaylord!' May fought back the desire to throw her arms round him and hug him to her. 'What *has* been happening?' And then she caught sight of him (they were in the jeep's headlights). 'Why, you're wet through!'

'Miles and I were fighting. We fell in the river.'

May was intrigued. A late member of the

276

Sixth, and a member of the Upper Fifth, so far forgetting their dignity as to fight! It was like hearing that two members of the Bench of Bishops had had a go at each other. She said, 'What were you fighting about?'

'He impugned your honour,' said her son.

'God bless my soul,' said May. She pondered. Then she said, 'Well, you go into the house and get those wet things off. You'll be frozen.' It was all she could think of.

But the fireman said, 'One moment, young man. Did *you* set that boat on fire? Deliberately?'

'Sort of,' said Gaylord.

'May one ask why?'

'I don't know really. I think it was a funeral pyre.'

'Whose?'

'I don't know,' said Gaylord, looking troubled. 'I really don't know, sir.'

May, with sudden inspiration, said, 'Liz, go with Gaylord. See he has a hot bath and gets warm.' She put an affectionate hand on the girl's shoulder. '*Cosset* him, my dear.'

'Very well, Mrs Pentecost,' said Liz. She and Gaylord set off into the darkness. May said, 'Now, officer. What do you want to know?'

But the fire was quenched. And the officer said, 'I never think it's much use trying to discover teenagers' motives. It's much the best just to accept their actions, and see to

277

the tidying up afterwards.'

Jocelyn looked at him with respect. 'You're a wise officer, if I may say so.'

'Thank you, sir.'

The firemen set about pulling what was left of *The Christine* into the shore, and making it fast. Amanda helped them eagerly.

May and Jocelyn went back to their car. The night returned to brooding dark and brooding silence.

May said, 'Whose funeral pyre?'

Jocelyn was silent. May said, 'His love? His friendship?'

'No. I don't think so,' said Jocelyn.

'What then?'

'No one will ever know. Least of all Gaylord. But – it could have been his boyhood.'

'You're a clever old bird,' said May. 'I never thought of that.'

'Better be going,' said Jocelyn. 'I'll call Amanda. Gaylord was in quite a state.'

'No hurry. Liz is quite capable, and she'll be in seventh heaven, fussing over him–'

'Or could it have been innocence?' mused Jocelyn.

'I don't think so.' She said, 'It's a strange thing, but I think Gaylord will never quite lose his innocence. I think – whatever he has to face – it will stay with him. A certain shield.'

Together they strolled back to the water's edge. The creatures of darkness had their night back. Somewhere in the shadow that covered half the earth a match had flared, and died.

Signifying–? Perhaps much, perhaps nothing. Perhaps a man joining the throng that presses along that unknown road, caught between galaxies and atoms, ecstasy and agony. Perhaps a boy, no longer running and laughing in the summer mornings, gone forever. May said, 'I hope Charles and his merry widow–'

'Yes. He's been a lonely man. And you? I mean, I know you liked him. You don't–?'

She hung on to his arm. 'What I like about writers,' she said, 'is the clarity with which they express themselves. No,' she said, 'Of course I don't.' And she thought: God, what a lesson I've had. All my life I've been a realist. My love has been real, my pity has been practical, my heart has been in the right place, I hope, but my head has always ruled it. And then, suddenly, a woman in her forties, I became awash with sentimentality because a man was in love with me and I pitied him and the years were passing forever. And instead of sending him packing I talked of comforting him, of taking him to my heart. And so I might, just might, if a bird hadn't fallen so strangely from the sky, and if tonight he hadn't slapped my face just as painfully as I slapped his. Yes, what a lesson! Thank goodness I've learnt it in time.

279

She said, 'But I *could* have made a fool of myself over old Charles.'

He thought this over. 'I don't think you could. Not you. Oh, I know it looks easy. But we're hemmed in, people like us.' He went on thinking. 'Or perhaps,' he said, 'it's like what you were just saying about Gaylord. A sort of – innocence.'

'I wonder,' she said. 'I really wonder.'

CHAPTER 18

So the stars looked down: on the tolerant, amused corner of England that the Pentecosts had created for themselves.

Old John Pentecost slept. He had known boyhood and manhood, marriage and bereavement, war and peace. He had seen his world changed more than any man before him had seen it change: from carts to cars to aeroplanes to supersonic jets. In his youth they had still been discovering bits of Africa. Now they were sifting the soil of Mars. He had seen men and women (or so it seemed to him) grow hard to match the steel and concrete that surrounded them; and the world's laughter had grown shrill, where it was not already silenced. He was glad he was old. He was glad he had spent the good years in the days when men and women were simple, and had a sort of innocence. He was glad he wasn't young Gaylord, on the threshold of a world so crammed with activity that few ever notice the hollowness within. Sleep, and forgetfulness: that was what suited an old man.

Amanda would not have shared his fears. For Amanda was not only interested in everything and everybody, she *loved* everything and everybody (except those unfortunates she hated with a most enjoyable hatred).

She was not unduly worried about her dear Roger's infatuation with the Rhine maiden, chiefly because in the last five minutes she'd fallen in love with a handsome young fireman called Reg. And, for the rest, there was all the eager joyousness of ten years old, and a complete faith in the rightness of things. She cartwheeled merrily home, under the cartwheeling heavens.

And for May and Jocelyn, the elastic band we call marriage was suddenly tight and snug again. They were together, held close. She had returned to him after unhappy wanderings. And so it was. The years lay ahead – comfortable, contented, with ups and downs that would always be bearable so long as they were together. Until the unthinkable days came when they *were* no longer together. But that must not be thought of. No. Her thoughts had strayed, she had known strange desires, she had swum in a warm and slumberous sea of temptation. But she had not swum far. What had Jocelyn said? A sort of innocence? Would that have saved her? Even without tonight's slap on the face?

She thought so. But she would never be sure. Only a fool would ever prophesy about human behaviour. And May Pentecost was no fool.

And the stars looked down on Gaylord Pentecost, and on Liz Bunting.

For lovers, the countryside at night is a fine and private place.

But what's the use of that, Liz Bunting thought bitterly, when the loved one is shivering violently, when the loved one is wet and dripping, when the loved one's teeth are beginning to chatter. 'Come on,' she said. 'Up to the house.'

'Must go and see what's happened to old Miles first,' he said.

'Gaylord, that's nonsense.'

'It isn't. He was lying by the river. He might slip back into the water, anything.'

She grabbed his sleeve, for a woman will cheerfully see the whole human race slip back into the water, provided the man she loves is safe.

But she could not hold him back. 'Listen,' she said angrily, 'Roger Miles will never come to any harm. He's got an ego like an inflatable life raft.'

He ignored her. But when they came to the little beach it was empty. 'What did I tell you?' said Liz. 'I bet he's at your house. I bet he's in your bath. By the time we get there he'll have used all the hot water. And I *did* want – while you had a nice long soak – to get you a nice hot supper, and now your mother will be there first to look after you and I shall be young Liz again and I shan't be able to do anything for you and you're going back to school tomorrow and I shan't see you till Christmas.' This remarkable and, to Gaylord, astonishing speech was delivered on a steadily rising note which became at the end almost a wail. And about half way through she began to drum on his chest, and continued at an ever-increasing tempo.

It was extraordinary. Young Liz had never behaved like this before. He didn't know what to say. Then he remembered something he had been going to tell her; something that would be rather a treat for her. He said, 'Er, talking about Christmas, Miles says I might be in the XV next term.'

She stopped drumming. She felt exhausted and ashamed and despairing. And almost as wet with tears as Gaylord was with river. She said, 'Oh, good. I'm ever so glad, Gaylord.'

'No,' he said. 'I wasn't telling you for that. Only – there's a fixture with Ingerby Grammar in November. At their place. I'd thought you might like to come and watch.'

'Gaylord, I'd love to.' But there was something she had to clarify. 'Had you meant to say this before I – made a fool of myself? You're not just saying it to cheer me up?'

'No. Honest. And you didn't make a fool of yourself. Old Miles – he's a marvellous chap, of course – but–' He spoke as though a great light had dawned on him – 'He *is* the sort of chap who'd use all a chap's bath water. You're right, Liz.'

They walked on in silence. 'So's Christine,' he said thoughtfully.

Liz said quietly, 'Perhaps we all are.'

'No,' he said. *'You're* not, Liz.' And sneezed violently.

'Really, Gaylord?' she said. She walked along by his side. His teeth were chattering properly, now, and she was still a bit sniffy and tearful. But she was curiously happy of a sudden. She was invited to stand in the November mud, and watch thirty young men play a game she would never understand if she lived to be a hundred. But she knew that for Gaylord this invitation was rather like bestowing a half of his kingdom on her.

And he had paid her a compliment. Oh, he hadn't said her eyes were like stars or her lips like rubies or her teeth like pearls. He'd just said she wasn't the sort of girl to pinch a chap's bath water. But that was enough to please Liz.

She trudged along. Young Liz Bunting, with her man, in the dark night; still blowing her nose, still dabbing her eyes.

But her head was crowned with stars.

This Large Print Book, for people
who cannot read normal print,
is published under the auspices of

THE ULVERSCROFT FOUNDATION